# THE WATCHMAKER'S APPRENTICE

CLAIRE FENNELL

ISBN: 978-0-578-41397-6

Book design by Wordzworth
*www.wordzworth.com*

This novel is dedicated to English teachers.
We owe you all far more credit than you recieve.

"Contrary to popular thinking,
being worthy isn't something you earn.
It's something you recognize."

–MIKE DOOLEY–

# Prologue

The old man sighed and sat up, straightening his spine as far as it would go despite years hunched over a desk as knotted as his muscles now were. He laid his pen on the surface of the wooden desk and twisted the cork back into the bottle of ink.

The paper he had been writing on made a slight swishing sound as he used it to fan the air, drying the last dredges of wet ink. He folded the paper carefully, running a crooked finger over each crease.

His finger protested the motion with a cry of pain, the changing weather granting his joints no particular favors. He ignored the cry, instead picking up the small box that sat beside the pen.

He situated the paper within the box, smoothed it out so it rested comfortably within its new home. It would be a long journey, he knew that much.

Journey, coming from the Old French word *journée,* meaning a day's work, his minimal knowledge of the language reminded him.

*A day's work.* The old man almost laughed as he placed the lid on the box, nailed it shut. A day?

*C'est un souhait.*

That is a wish.

# CHAPTER ONE

The intrigue of Gillonsville was not that it was inherently intriguing, but rather that it had somehow managed to maintain its lack of intrigue for a startlingly extensive period of time. This lack of intrigue had a relatively boundless reach, one with enough breadth to thoroughly and completely blanket Gillonsville Junior High.

It's funny how frequently one's mind turns to the boredom of a place when surrounded by nothing but bare concrete. The structure I was sitting on was a sort of amphitheater that grew outrageously cold in the winter and outrageously hot in the summer, ensuring that it was never actually enjoyable.

It was purchased by the PTA as an outdoor classroom, a general failure considering it was A) never used for school purposes and B) never really used for any purpose at all, besides a relatively secluded lunch spot.

In October, as it was today, the cold of the concrete seeped through my jeans, and I shrugged my cream-colored sweater more tightly around my shoulders.

"Oh. My. God."

I looked up, matching a familiar cry with a familiar face. Isaac, one of the few interesting things about our barely-worth-putting-on-a-map town.

He swung his backpack off of his shoulder and onto the concrete with anger that didn't match his too-lanky form and almost-oversized tortoiseshell glasses. "Mr. Capill should quit his job – actually, no, be *fired* immediately." He reached into his backpack and pulled out a PB&J.

I sighed. "So how was the math test?"

"Take a guess," he said through a sticky bite. "About as well as every invasion of Russia, save that of the Mongols."

"Isaac Collins, you are such a nerd."

"As if you aren't, Kelsey *Jacobson*."

Isaac ran his hand through his curly hair as he laughed, his smile brighter than the fabric of his light gray t-shirt.

I laughed too, reaching into my backpack and producing a lunch of my own. I unwrapped my sandwich slowly, deliberately salvaging the foil only to crumple it into a ball when it was fully removed. I set the ball aside and chewed carefully.

I raised my sandwich to take another bite, but was cut off by a voice calling from the doorway to the school. "Kelsey, Isaac. Come here."

Genevieve Villanueva's eyes always carried an ambitious spark as wild as her hair, but that day it was different. Less driven, simply… Curious.

Isaac held up his sandwich, raised it in protest. Gen groaned. "Come on, Isaac!" she said emphatically. "You can eat your PB&J whenever. This is *important*."

Isaac begrudgingly set the sandwich aside, zipped it into his backpack as Gen tapped her foot impatiently. He swung the bag over his shoulder, walking at a pace that was too slow, at least so far as I could discern from Gen's expression.

The moment we were close enough, Gen clamped her hand around my arm, pulling me along with her in a way that could only be described as dragging. Isaac followed as Gen pulled me through the hallway, me muttering apologies as I collided with the other students drifting past.

Gen suddenly took a hard left into the janitor's closet, the door snapping shut behind her after she half-ushered half-pushed me and Isaac inside.

"Gen, what is this?" Isaac said. I groaned as I rubbed my arm where she had gripped it. Isaac moved to flip over an orange Home Depot bucket, transforming it into a stool as per his usual habit during our janitor's closet conferences.

Gen shrugged. "Sorry, sorry, but you will not *believe* what I just found."

At this, the small wooden box she clutched in her hands became apparent to me for the first time. The box looked ancient, the nails no more than pillars of weathered rust, suspended by sheer willpower.

I raised my eyebrows. "What is that, and when was your last tetanus shot?"

"Whatever," she deflected, though I noticed her thumb jumped slightly away from the nail. "Anyways, it *might* just be a prank." She then smiled, and declared, "I don't think it is. This seems different." She paused for a moment as we heard high-heeled footsteps outside the closet. We held our collective breath, not daring to exhale until the sound had passed.

Students couldn't care less about our presence here. Teachers, on the other hand? Well, it serves to say we had been caught before, and detention, although not a punishment of medieval proportions, was not the most fun way to spend a Saturday.

Once we were sure the footsteps had fully faded, Gen spoke again. "Ok, false alarm. Anyways, listen to this."

She opened the box, wincing slightly when one of the nails crumbled into dust as she pulled the lid away. She extracted a folded paper from the bottom of the wooden container and began to read aloud.

*Dear Reader,*

*I would like to hope this letter ends up in good hands, for I fear what may happen if not. The first thing you should know is that the stuff of stories, the things adults may write off as child's play, at least to some extent, is real. Choose not to believe me if you must, simply put the box back and I will wait for someone else to pursue this opportunity. Go to Montague and Sons' Watchmakers. I assume you know of it. On the back wall count the 18th brick down, 11th brick over. Behind this you will find answers, and if you are who I think you are, you will become something greater than you could ever imagine yourselves being, something, dare I say, almost magical.*

*Regards,*

*P.Q.M.*

Gillonsville's previous reason for intrigue was faltering, but I couldn't say the replacement was unsatisfactory. The weight of P.Q.M.'s words sat thickly in the air of the closet, almost tangible. Gen refolded the note, smoothed out the edges, once, twice, three times. She turned it over as if trying to divulge some truth from its mass, its weight in her hands.

"So, what's the verdict? Reality or prank?"

I laughed dryly. "Reality? Gen, it says magic is real. As cool as that sounds…" I trailed off.

"Normally I would agree with you," Gen said, and Isaac snorted. "But why would anyone bother? The amount of effort it would take to fake how old this box is… It wouldn't be worth it to someone our age. And an adult certainly wouldn't write it."

"Why not?" Isaac asked, scrunching his nose.

She looked at him as though his lack of intelligence was a personal attack. "Were you listening? *The things adults might write off as child's play.* It's simple. Adults *never* admit they're wrong."

Isaac nodded slowly. "You're asking the wrong kind of question, then. The real question is what kind of person would legitimately do this?"

"Someone who means it, obviously," Gen said, rolling her eyes on the last word.

"But, I mean… it's crazy, right?" Isaac sounded as though he was asking himself as much as anyone else.

"Is that worth the chance that it isn't?"

Gen and Isaac both turned to me, their eyes both wide.

Isaac had a point. I didn't believe it either, not at first. But then Gen, in her patent manner, had me questioning that conviction.

*Crazy.* The word reverberated in my ears. Maybe it was. In fact, it most definitely was. But crazy and wrong? Those words are not synonyms. It was this which pushed the words through my lips, startling even me.

The second time I spoke, it wasn't a question.

"Let's do it."

It was the next day, and I was seated across from Isaac and Gen in a booth at our usual rendezvous, Kelly's Diner.

The buzz of the fan reminded me of long afternoons drinking Diet Coke out of sweating bottles, always occupying the booth second closest to the pane-glass window the summer after Isaac's triplet siblings were born and he didn't care where he was so long as it wasn't home. Then there was the jukebox, bleating a scratchy version of American Pie which we would dance to when Gen needed a break from her French homework, or when Isaac and I needed a break from quizzing her on the conjugations of être.

Today, school work was the least of our concerns, a rather surprising foray for the ever-studious Gen, who watched me intently as I spoke in hushed tones over my vanilla milkshake.

"So when do you guys want to do this?"

"Thursday?" Gen responded tentatively. "My mom'll be on a business trip, and though she'll flip a lid if she finds out, my dad won't notice, or at least won't care."

I nodded, then looked to Isaac. He was wearing a pale-blue t-shirt with a red paint stain on the sleeve. He grabbed a fry from the basket in the center of the table, and spoke with his mouth full of potato. "My parents couldn't care less. I could probably go live in Walmart for a week and they wouldn't even bat an eye. The three stooges are keeping them busy."

I coughed on a sip of milkshake as I laughed. "Three stooges is a new one," I said, dipping a french fry into my shake before popping it into my mouth, relishing the way the salt danced with the sweet.

Isaac grimaced. "Gross, Kels. But seriously, they're unbearable. Suddenly tweedle-dee, tweedle-dum, and tweedle dumber come along and I'm as obsolete as, I don't know, Crocs or something."

"Both of your opinions are incorrect," Gen said. "Fries plus milkshake – good. Crocs – godly. But I digress. Your brothers are two years old!"

"Oh yeah," Isaac scoffed, "easy for you to say. Try living with them!" He gave an over-exaggerated shudder. "Why did it have to be triplets?"

"Anyways," I interjected, raising my voice ever-so slightly. "Thursday at midnight?"

Gen pulled away from her straw, then swallowed, nodding, and Isaac gave a thumbs up with one hand, the other occupied with a fry.

I laughed harshly. "When did our lives come to this? Midnight plans to break into a – Hi, Mr. Kelly!"

He smiled warmly. "Something I should know about?"

His tone was parental, and from anyone else I would have found it condescending, but not from him. With how much time we spent at the diner, it was basically his right.

"All good, Mr. K," I said, with my best 'totally-not-going-to-break-into-an-abandoned-building-on-Thursday' smile.

"Well in any case," he said, tucking a strand of his blond hair behind his ear, "This round's on me."

Gen opened her mouth to protest, but Mr. Kelly just held up a silencing hand, smiling warmly. "I insist."

"Thanks," Isaac called, as the familiar green aproned figure began to depart.

"Of course," Mr. Kelly called over his shoulder. "Plus," he added, pausing to grin back at Isaac, "I'm sure you'll be back next week."

My throat suddenly felt thick, and it wasn't because of the milkshake.

Twelve came on Thursday with the presumptuously mild anticipation of an event which had lost the shine of its excitement due to unprecedentedly boring classes during an unprecedentedly boring three days of school. I stood under the lone street light a few doors down from the watchmaker's, hands in my pockets, my arms crossed tight over my chest in something that was not defense, but rather the most primitive version of the gesture. It was cold, and the slight wind teased the air through my hair.

Isaac leaned against the exposed brick wall across from me, checking his phone with sporadic periodicity. Gen was late, something outside of her usual realm of color coded planners and highlighted calendars.

I was too lost in thought to notice the painfully slow passage of time as we waited for Gen, my demeanor uncharacteristically introspective. I just couldn't fathom it... Why was the watchmaker's there? I cast it a sideways glance and tried to recall any sort of past that it had in my mind. I failed. It wasn't in business in my lifetime, I knew that, but there could have been other purposes – a gala, an elementary school field trips, even auctions – but there weren't. It didn't have purpose, only mass.

Maybe it was one of those places every small town has, its irrelevance a product of its consistency. As everything around it was being torn down, built up, reshaped, reinvented, its static nature was being shrouded by the dynamic.

We heard Gen before we saw her that night – somewhere close to half-past twelve – her breath heavy even in the thin air. Her run slowed to a jog which slowed to a stop and she leaned next to Isaac on the wall.

"Sorry," she said airily. "Dad was up late."

*Montague and Son's Watchmaker's. Est. 1800.*

Six words on a slightly swinging black and gold sign shone, illuminated by the soft yellow glow of the moonlight. Although rationale told me I had seen the shop before, I felt as if I was seeing it for the first time.

"Well, here goes nothing," Isaac declared, his nonchalant tone masking the weight of the words.

*Here goes everything,* I thought.

Isaac reached out and clasped the rusted bronze knob, twisting it harshly. His hand slipped, and he hissed as the rust grated against his bare skin.

"Here," Gen said, stepping forward. She too clasped the knob, gave it an equally driven tug. Nothing. "It's stuck. Actually-" She tugged again, frowning as the knob twisted slightly but didn't give. "It's locked."

"Yeah, thanks, for the FYI Genevieve," Isaac said, rubbing his palm. "I had no idea."

She looked at him pointedly, before turning to me, her

expression somewhat softer. "Any ideas?"

I held up my hands. "Don't ask me."

She exhaled slowly, and I could see the cogs turning in her mind, smoothly and rhythmically. The streetlight's glow brought her in and out of the light as she paced. She stopped and her face lit up despite being in shadow.

Pulling her phone out of her pocket, she began typing frantically. I had always found the clicking of her keyboard somewhat obnoxious, and its harsh nature was nothing if not highlighted in the quiet dark.

She scrolled through what I imagined to be search results, making little noises of dissent. "No… no… Maybe?" She was silent for a minute, her eyes flicking across the small screen. "No." Her scrolling slowed down, and she paused, her motion quelling. "This one."

She held the screen up to me, and I squinted against the bright square of light for a moment before the article came into focus.

I laughed. "Gen."

"Do you have any better ideas?"

I stared at the phone, scanning the article. "No," I relented.

The words *HOW TO PICK A LOCK* stared back at me, innocently sinister.

"We're *so* going to get in trouble," Isaac lamented, as Gen handed me a gift card from her favorite bookstore with a cry of – "You better not break this! I've had my eye on a Harry Potter box set for weeks now."

How I had been chosen to play the role of "breaking" in breaking and entering, I was unsure, but somehow I found myself with the card in one hand and Gen's phone in the other.

I read the rest of the article, published on an exceedingly sketchy website, the kind of sketchy that included the symbol for anarchy emblazoned on the top corner in blood red. The maneuver seemed simple enough really.

*Slide the card into the crack.*

*Tilt the card towards the knob.*

*Bend the card back the opposite way.*

The lock popped open.

I turned back to face my friends, and handed Gen back her card and phone. "Ok, so I am now *officially* James Bond."

"Oh, whatever," Isaac said, although I sensed a hint of jealousy in his words.

The serenity of the otherwise silent October night was broken as I twisted the bronze door knob, releasing an almost human shriek from the depths of the arthritic mechanisms.

"This is ludicrous," Gen whispered.

My stubborn nature told me Gen had to be wrong, we weren't crazy, try as my logic might to plead to the contrary. *Logic* reminded me our small posse of thirteen-year-olds had no business breaking into long abandoned watchmaker's, in our barely-worth-putting-on-a-map Connecticut town.

However, my stubbornness won the debate, rendering any argument to the contrary entirely obsolete.

As I pushed the thick oak door open I stepped inside, the other's following, and we paused for a moment, allowing our eyes to adjust to the half-light from the outside street lamps filtering in through a moderately grimy window.

The whole shop smelled old, the sort of mix of wood and mothballs and a few other unidentifiable things everyone with grandparents knows.

I walked to my right, running my hand along the glass cases which lined the room on either side. My hand came away coated with dust, and I peered through the small window I had made, barely able to discern row upon row of watches through the remaining grime.

I reached the far end of the shop and studied a large wooden desk, and not the IKEA kind; Something coming before IKEA was even the slightest inkling of an idea in anyone's mind, something not of this era. No, the desk was more the kind belonging in a museum, behind bulletproof glass almost as thick as the wood itself.

Beyond the desk was what we had come for: A wall of bricks reaching from floor to ceiling, almost identical to the wall Isaac and Gen had been leaning against.

"Eighteen down, eleven over," Isaac muttered as his hands traced their way across the bricks. He curled his long fingers around the edges of the brick, his lips turning down at the corners. He tugged sharply and stumbled backwards as he lost his grasp.

Gen smirked. "This might help." She produced a small silver switchblade from the pocket of her jeans.

How she had gotten her hands on it, I had no idea.

It had been challenge enough for her to sneak out at this hour which, I concluded, glancing at my phone screen, was growing later and later with every minute. The anticipation was a jolt of caffeine, though, keeping the minutes from tiring me.

She rolled her eyes, then passed me the blade. I moved past Isaac to stand in front of the wall, and gently slid the knife into the space where the brick met the mortar. I sawed around the perimeter of the brick, gritting my teeth as the knife scraped against the wall.

"Care to do the honors?"

Isaac swooned mockingly. "The great James Bond letting me play MI6? Of course!"

I moved to trade places with him once more, and he re-situated his fingers around the brick. The three of us drew in our breath in almost perfect unison, and Isaac tugged.

He pulled forward, then, when that failed, began to shift it from side to side. He had retrieved an approximate half-inch of brick before it refused to budge once more. He sighed, and pushed it back in slightly before pulling away sharply. The brick and mortar ground against each other as the brick popped free. A cloud of dust swelled from around the opening, and I pulled my shirt over my face.

The heavy sound was followed by a harsh clatter of metal against stone as the evidently hollowed-out brick was relieved of its contents.

A note with scrawling ink winked up at us from the stone ground. Isaac bent down and scooped up the spilled objects, depositing them on the thick wooden desk.

I plucked the note from the table and held it up to the mild light.

"Put them on," I read, my tone terse. I inhaled sharply "Signed… PQM." The note looked impossibly old, with jet-black ink bearing a sharp contrast to the faded yellow parchment it was stained upon. The handwriting was the same loopy yet refined script we had seen a few days ago in the janitor's closet.

Our collective vision turned slowly toward the desk and the items gently transitioned into clarity for the first time.

There lay three watches, one gold, one silver, and one bronze, each with a purple fleur-de-lis in the place of the twelve on their faces. The purple stones glowed with a disproportionate amount of light considering the lack of such glow in the room as a whole.

It was as if the light was not being reflected off of the smoothly cut gems, but rather emanating from somewhere deep within them. The gold was warm, almost sunny. It reminded me of the gold of my mother's wedding ring, and I felt a tinge of longing. The silver was sleek, worthy of James Bond. The bronze was inviting and almost humble, the same color as a freshly minted penny.

These watches… Their beauty was intrinsic, inexplicably ever-present. It was not their beauty that amazed me, though, it was this innate feeling of connection. I couldn't explain the way the watches made me feel. The awe crushed my chest, made my lungs feel tight. I was not afraid, although I felt all the usual symptoms: palms sweaty, breath and heart both quickened… Instead I felt elevated, almost, in the strangest way. This was bigger than me, bigger than Isaac or Gen or all of us combined. This was real.

Isaac reached out first, grabbing the bronze watch from the table. He turned it over in his hands a few times, although he made no move to look at it. Gen moved next, clutching the gold watch with a fist tight enough that only a half moon of gold peeked through the crack of her hand.

I picked up the silver and ran my hand along the strap. It felt cold under my fingers, despite the warm glow of the emerald. I shivered, although I didn't think it to be related to the temperature of the metal.

"What's our playbook here?" Isaac, clearly, was able to break his enamourment far faster than me.

"Uh…" I tried to speak, but I my words merely sputtered then ceased, the vehicle of my thoughts breaking down.

"Are we going to listen? And put them on, I mean." Isaac's voice trailed off, taking on a tentative hitch.

"Why not?"

Gen's phrasing amused me, the casual flippancy the same as that expressed over a decision on what board game to play, what movie to watch. Despite my amusement, however, I felt comforted by the normalcy, and nodded.

"Let's do it."

We slipped the watches onto our wrists, the air filled with mumbles of frustration as we finagled our respective clasps into place.

There was a pregnant silence after the watches were secured. The silence was all encompassing -no hum of a passing car outside, no barking dog, no crunch of gravel, no cough- just a definitionally complete silence that rested upon us like a heavy blanket, limiting but reassuring.

"Nothing happened," Gen suddenly said, a slight edge sneaking into her voice.

"I don't understand." I looked down at my watch, willing it to do something, anything.

"Well, I'm calling it," Isaac interjected, his tone surprisingly calm. "That was the definition of an anticlimax, and I-" Isaac stopped mid-sentence and looked down at his watch, eyes frantic. The watch's previously tame glow now burned with that of a thousand suns, urgently and unforgivingly.

I looked to my own wrist and saw the same overbearing glow. Within a few seconds the glow occupied the entirety of the room, and my eyes burned with the contrast. Just as the glow reached its climax and spots danced across my vision, multiplying until they entirely obscured it, I felt myself being yanked up by the wrist like a marionette, bending to the whim of an unknown puppeteer.

# CHAPTER TWO

The feeling of being lifted was coupled with a painfully fascinating sensation, one that made me feel as though I was being squeezed through a soda bottle while simultaneously being sliced apart as if I were butter. I screwed my eyes shut against it, but before I could will my way through it, it was over and I once again felt blessedly solid ground through the soles of my yellow converse.

I hesitantly opened my eyes. I looked at my hands and wiggled my fingers, clenched and unclenched my fists. The reassurance of a working-order body lent me the will to examine my surroundings. We were still in the watchmaker's, I could discern that much. At least, I thought I could.

While the desk was still in the same place, and the walls were still lined with glass-paneled cases, they had lost their aged, antique look. The glass was clear, sparkling without so much as a memory of dust. An array of watches was meticulously placed on the plush purple velvet interior of the cases, sparkling in the same manner. The desk looked recently polished, and even the floor seemed to have been swept not long ago.

The only true constant was the light through the raised window which still cast ghostly shadows against the cobblestone floor. I squinted, though, noticing a change in the quality of the light. I soon realized why as I traced the light. It was no longer coming from a street light, as there were no street lights to be seen. The only source I could discern was a crescent moon.

I turned to Gen and Isaac, noticing them for what felt like the first time. "Does this look off to you?"

Gen nodded, sounding like she was chasing her breath as it tried to escape her. "Wait." She drew her wrist upward, pulling back the sleeve of her hoodie. She looked down then clasped her hand over her mouth, a whispered *no* slipping between her fingers.

I wordlessly pulled up my own sleeve, feeling as though my eyes were pressing against the glass face of the watch despite the space that separated them. "You're kidding."

Isaac's exclamation came seconds after mine. "*Impossible.*"

I blinked, scrubbed my eyes, looked again. Nothing had changed, and the phrase illuminated in the faint traces of light sent electricity staggering through my veins.

The dial on the watches, the one that only minutes ago read 2018 had changed. A new date had taken its place.

*1811.*

It couldn't be true. It had to be a fluke, some magnetic irregularity.

The notes, the box, the watches… None of it could be true.

Isaac and Gen's faces fell slack.

"I'm not the only one seeing this, right?" Isaac said, his voice rattling like spare change in a tin can.

Gen nodded. "1811?"

Isaac opened his mouth as if to speak, then closed it soundlessly.

"We're in 1811." The words felt heavy as they rolled from my tongue.

Isaac laughed harshly. "Expect the unexpected, I guess."

"Unexpected? It's your past! There's nothing much more predictable than that."

All three of us turned abruptly as a voice of a different caliber entered the room.

I froze, squinting into the dimness, attempting to make out the figure who had been watching us from the darkness. Nothing creeped me out more than feeling like I was being watched.

I felt as though I was one of those bugs- like the ones I saw in the Smithsonian on a fourth grade field trip -trapped in amber whether they liked it or not.

"What? Cat got your tongue?" The voice moved closer. "I think it's fair to assume you three found the note, then?"

Gleaming eyes – were they purple? – were the first thing to emerge from the shadows, peering at us through bottle-cap spectacles, studying us.

"I must say, I had higher hopes for you three, making it all the way back here, then being stunned into silence by a crotchety old man such as myself."

At this, the darkness relinquished the rest of the form.

"Sorry?" Isaac's stuttered remark was met with a surprisingly reassuring snicker from the old man as he lit one of the oil lamps adorning the walls, bathing the room in a yellow glow.

"Don't be sorry, just be logical. Look at me!" He spread his arms. I had to admit, he was right. He was remarkably unformidable with his wispy grey hair which looked as if a cloud had chosen to take up residence upon his head. His wrinkled bony frame was adorned with a black cloth smock tied neatly around his waist.

I shifted awkwardly.

"So, who exactly are you?" Gen said in an impressively steady voice.

The man drummed his knotted fingers against the thick wooden desk. "Again, be logical."

He crossed the room to a bookshelf filled with long narrow boxes, their ends marked with the same script-like handwriting from the notes. The old man selected a box from the shelf and placed it on the large desk. I squinted again, attempting but failing to make out the writing.

He gave us another pointed look. "You truly don't know?"

My jaw stiffened slightly. "You're not… *PQM?*"

"There's the brain I bargained for!" the man said excitedly.

His phrasing startled me. *Bargained for?*

He continued before I could finish my thought. "Yes, I'm PQM, in the colloquial sense. *Peter Q. Montague.* You can call me Mr. Montague, Peter, anything you like, although I must admit I'm rather opposed to Pete. I've always despised shortenings which only remove one letter. Who's so busy as to–"

"So, you wrote the letters?" Although I had only met the man, I was too excited to have reservations about cutting him off.

"Another stroke of brilliance!" He laughed once more, and it sounded like rusted wind-chimes.

I hoped the flush rising into my pale cheeks could be attributed to the cold.

"And your names are…" I felt as if I were watching some sort of children's television program, the kind that asked too-simple questions too slowly then trailed off into a too-long pause.

"Oh. Sorry." A nod and a frown from Peter told me all I needed to know his feelings regarding my repetition of the phrase. "I'm Kelsey, that's Gen, and he's Isaac."

He nodded slowly, deliberately. "Kelsey. Gen. Isaac. Strong names."

I considered responding but instead I let out a yawn, then covered my mouth sheepishly.

Peter chuckled. "Should we be heading to your rooms, then?"

"Rooms? What? No, we shouldn't be heading to our rooms. We should be telling us where we are! What is this place? Why do our watches say 1811? Why are you dressed like a someone who lost a Game of Thrones costume contest at Comic Con?"

"Gen!" Isaac hissed. He lowered his voice to a whisper. "Calm down. You can't yell at old people. Especially 200-year-old people!"

Peter laughed. 'I'm not 200 years old, not yet any who. And I'm also not deaf, in fact I have excellent hearing, so don't bother whispering. Of course, you have questions. I suppose I could answer a few, but we will have to save some for tomorrow. As much as I resent admitting such things, my body is not what it used to be, and a man never truly outgrows the need for a hearty slumber. Come with me."

Peter straightened his hunched form slightly and loped toward the door, one leg dragging slightly behind, it being the silver medalist of the pair.

"Do you want a hand?" Isaac offered.

Peter shook his head with a smile as he heaved open a thick wooden door embedded in the brick wall at the back of the shop. "It's nothing more than a slight chink in my armor." The twinkle in his eyes turned briefly matte, as if a star were pulled into a black hole. "I've handled much worse at my old age."

I stepped a bit closer to Gen before I followed him.

"How did we get here?" I suddenly blurted.

Peter paused his limping stride. "Well, the watches, of course."

I felt like I was facing a sphinx.

Gen clicked her tongue impatiently. "But *how*?"

Peter began to walk again, and we reached a specific point in the candle lit hallway that made the white cloud of his hair turn stormy. "All in good time."

Gen bit her lip, quickening her pace until she was beside Peter. "Are the watches some kind of particle accelerator? Of course, the physics is next to impossible, unless you've found a way to travel faster than the speed of light, or–" she gasped suddenly "–you haven't figured out how to travel at negative speeds, have you?"

Isaac leans in towards me. "What the heck is a negative speed and why does Gen even know about it?" He rolled his eyes. "Nerd."

"So not the point right now Isaac!" I scolded as I strained to hear Peter's response.

Despite the barrage of questions, Peter's patience didn't falter. "It's not so much about physics, my dear."

"Then what *is* it?" Gen sped up once more until she was walking backwards in front of Peter.

"Genevieve," Peter said calmly, pausing in his stride. "You only ask so many questions because you are afraid you will not understand, yes?"

Gen nodded, uncharacteristically self-conscious.

"This is ill-founded. I promise you, you will understand when the time is right. The three of you–" he gestured collectively "–are far too intelligent to ever fail to learn something I have taught you."

"How do you know?" This was one question I couldn't resist asking.

"Well, you listened, did you not?"

We walked for another minute in relative silence, relaxed by the soft glow of the candle-lined hallway.

Peter hauled open one door, than walked a few more paces and hauled open the adjacent one. "Ladies," he gestured, "and gentleman." His smile brushed a twinkle across his eyes, and I noticed he was standing almost directly beneath a candle. "It is late, and as Isaac so observantly noted, I am old. We all need rest. Sleep now and we will speak more in the morning."

"Thank you," I said, suddenly hyper-aware of every nuance of my facial expression. I tried to smile back, and although my muscles cooperated, I felt as if my facade was incredibly obvious.

I was jealous of how easily Peter's aura of sincerity was maintained as he nodded us into the room with a goodnight and a promise of further explanations to come.

Gen and I hadn't even bothered to lie when we entered the room. We simply perched on the corner of the bed and waited for the knock. A few moments later, there was a soft tapping on our door. I stood and opened it, ushering Isaac into the room.

The edge of the bed bowed slightly as we resumed our perch.

Gen sighed. "So."

"This doesn't seem safe." Isaac chewed on his lip as he paused. "I mean, Peter could be *anyone*. I don't think it's safe to trust him."

"I just think we're out of our league," I offered. "Do you really think we're capable of doing what he does? Whatever that is. I mean, it seems pretty special."

Gen nodded. "He said we were, you heard him just as well as I did. Capability isn't my worry. I see where Isaac is coming from, though. We have no idea how to get home."

A feeling of dread began to creep around the edges of my awareness. Although we had the whole world around us, we were stuck. I swallowed hard, and stole myself. "We need to figure that out before we commit to anything. We're just being stupid otherwise."

"Simple enough," Gen said, a smile spreading across her face. "We tell him we'll help him, but he has to give us a fail safe. He can't say no, not really. We're no use to him if he can't get us to do what he wants."

Isaac still looked slightly uneasy, shifting in his seat, but I was placated. I was ready for adventure. It was only being trapped that scared me.

"*Please,* Isaac." Now Gen was practically begging, her tone bordering on a whine. "Home is so boring. We have the chance to have an adventure. A real one. Not just band practice, or the diner. We have the chance to do something that matters." Gen studied each of us in turn. "Any objections?"

Isaac paused, blew out a long breath, then shook his head. "No, no. I guess you're right." He took off his glasses and pinched the bridge of his nose. "If we have a way out, and he gives us a way to get home, yes, let's do it. Plus,–" this time he smiled "–with the triplets to occupy them, my family will barely even notice I'm gone."

Gen turned to me now. "Kels?"

"Like Isaac said. You give us a fail safe, and I'm in."

"Good." She said the word with an air of finality. "In that case, Peter is right. We'll be useless tomorrow without sleep. We need to rest."

It was dark enough, and Gen and I were tired enough, for us to take no notice of the room, instead opting to simply blow out the few candles dotting the walls, then collapse fully clothed into comically plush queen mattress as soon as Isaac exited.

Admittedly, my exhaustion did not stem far enough to quiet my thoughts into sleep.

My thoughts were captive within my brain but they were still left with plenty of space to wander. I turned from my back onto my side, trying to sway my mental state, but to little avail. In the moment, I was trapped. I was filled with the childish adrenaline coming from doing something not wrong, but also far from right. When sleep did come, it did not come smoothly.

When the Grecian army delivered the horse to Troy, they waited to attack. Isaac told me that, once upon a time before some history test I hadn't bothered studying for. Their stalling was a perfectly justified military tactic, he had said excitedly, luring the Trojan's into an ignorant false sense of security, real life dramatic irony. Despite this, basic human instincts would have commanded them to attack.

Most history books suggest there were about thirty people in the horse. So what made all thirty of those people sit in silence, waiting in a way that left them measuring their breaths?

I didn't get it then, but now the answer was suddenly plain to me. It was because their ability to do so wasn't guaranteed, and because there was a chance nothing would ever be guaranteed again

# CHAPTER THREE

When Peter collected us from our rooms the next morning, breakfast commenced quickly and left nothing to be desired. I spread some butter onto a piece of bread, trying to look diplomatic despite my nearly insatiable hunger.

Isaac, however, did not have as many reservations about attempting to look polite, and he was effectively stuffing his face with oatmeal.

"So, Peter," Gen said in between bites. "What exactly did you mean in your letter when you said 'magical?'"

I could tell by her tone that she was fighting to keep the hopeful note out of her voice.

Peter paused in the fixing of his coffee, his eyes developing a mischievous gleam.

"You all seem sharp enough. Think about why you're here. What kind of magic could have created these circumstances? Kelsey, any theories?"

I chewed slowly, stalling. "Well, we traveled in time,"

"And it started when we put on the watches," Gen interjected.

"So," I paused to glance down at the silver device still adorning my wrist. "You make… watches that time travel?"

"Essentially yes," Peter responded. "Control time, send people back, send people forwards, the works!"

"So basically Back to the Future, but with watches?" Isaac inquired.

"I can't say I'm entirely sure what that is, but you'll be able to decide for yourself soon enough."

"Meaning, what, exactly?" Isaac's voice rippled with energy.

"Meaning," Peter replied, his lips turning up at the corners, "that I'm going to teach you how to make them."

Our trio exchanged excited glances, and Isaac's coffee – if you could even call it that with the amount of milk and sugar he had dumped in – splashed over the rim of his mug, dripping onto his shaking hands. He drank it to feel intellectual, something I knew but he would never admit, an irony I couldn't help but consider as he hastily toweled off his hands.

"Before you ask anymore questions however, I have one for you." Peter spoke once more, breaking us out of our ecstatic trance.

"Anything!" Gen blushed with the realization that the word had been practically shouted.

"What exactly is the future like?"

"Well, wouldn't you know?" I asked, setting down my bread.

He developed the same look of confusion on all of our faces. "What do you mean?"

"I mean, you would have gone forward in time to deliver the note, right?" I said.

"Surprisingly, no." Peter read our expressions and continued. "Most people think of time in a strictly linear fashion, with events happening one at a time in a set sequence. But really, time is happening all at once. As I'm pouring my coffee here, the Mayflower could be arriving at Plymouth Rock a few miles east. Independence is entirely imagined. Neither event is truly separate, we're just trapped somewhere in the cycle. Think of it like this. When a spider traps a fly, the fly only knows the part of the web it inhabits. By no means does this negate the existence of the rest of the web. These watches,–" –he held up his wrist– "–they make us the spider." He paused. "Therefore, when I decided I needed an apprentice, or *apprentices* in this case," he corrected, gesturing to us with his fork as he paused in his cutting of a piece of bacon. "I simply passed the note on to someone else, and told them to pass it along as well. Due to the way time behaves, a note given to someone in 1811 with the instructions to be passed along to 2017 would appear there at the exact moment I passed it to the first person."

I could feel my brow crease. "But why do you need apprentices at all? And couldn't you find anyone in 1811 to work with? Why did you need to pull us out of our time into yours?"

Peter shifted his gaze from me, down to his coffee. As he lifted his mug to his lips he murmured, "All in good time."

"That's what you said last night," I pressed. "Now seems as good a time to me as any. Ow!—" I winced as Gen kicked me under the table. *Shut up!* she mouthed, sliding her eyes from me to Peter. The way he looked at me over his mug was unnerving and indecipherable. Not menacing so much as it was... concerned, almost.

Ever the diplomat, Isaac changed the subject. "So, what you're basically saying is, Abraham Lincoln is being assassinated as we speak?"

"Who?"

Gen looked at Isaac, eyes wide.

"Never mind," he admonished, "forget I said anything."

Peter's expression gave no indication he had any intention of forgetting. I didn't think it would matter, really. If we could come here without posing any danger, what was the real threat to knowing about the future? I made a mental note to ask the question later, filing under a number of more pressing questions.

"As it *seems*," I cringed slightly at the inflection Peter put on the word, "you get the concept, now can you tell me what 2018 is like?"

His tone almost made him sound like an overeager toddler, and I covered my mouth for a moment, stifling a chuckle.

"Well... We have machines now that allow us to talk to people thousands of miles away."

I paused to give him time to process this, but he waved me on with a piece of toast.

"And, there's this thing called the internet, which is..."

I trailed off, looking to my friends for help. *How do you explain the internet to someone who hasn't even seen a car yet?*

Gen picked up the slack. "It's kind of like, well, imagine an entire library, with all the knowledge in the world, condensed into one thing that can fit inside a shoebox."

"Fascinating," Peter rubbed his chin, "Absolutely fascinating."

"Hold on a second." Gen placed her mug down and pushed her hair behind her ears. "If you're so curious, why don't you just go yourself?"

"The same reason I can't tell you three everything you want to know just yet. And the same reason I need apprentices."

Now he really had Gen hooked. "And why exactly is that?" Her eyes shone.

He sighed. "Genevieve. I am no stranger to your intelligence, so I expect you know the old saying regarding absolute power."

"Absolute power corrupts absolutely. Lord Acton." Isaac barely whispered the words.

"Ah, yes," Peter said, smiling. "Mr. Collins. Our historian. I should have known. Yes, absolute power corrupts absolutely."

Gen leaned impossibly farther forward. "But why does it apply?"

"This power of mine – the time travel, I mean – is not without consequence. And if it becomes absolute, or if one wishes for it to be, the fallout is most unfortunate."

"But we're not wishing for power. We're just curious."

Gen said the statement as though it were the most obvious thing in the world.

Peter winced.

Isaac's eyes flooded with concern. "What?"

"This is not the first time I have heard such a statement. He said the same, just before…" Peter suddenly broke into a rather unnatural smile. "Well, I mustn't worry you. With the proper precautions, there's no reason we wouldn't be fine."

"Peter," I said slowly. "What happened with… 'him.'"

His smile flickered in and out, as though it were losing its signal. He finally dropped it completely. "I suppose it does me no good to leave you completely in the dark. And Aesop will have my head if I don't occasionally admit the need for a cautionary fable." His face darkened. "You three are not my first apprentices. He… he was the first. He came in with glistening curiosity. Eager, willing to learn. He was every teacher's dream."

"Then what?" Gen bit in.

"Then–" Peter paused. "Then he wasn't. Things were not as they should have been. When I look within these watches, I see a tool. A tool for helping others. This apprentice, on the other hand, only saw his own reflection. A tool for helping himself. His ambition ran away, and later, he did the same."

"Well," Isaac said, voice shaking, "where is he now?"

Peter's unnatural expression cut back across his face. "So, watchmaking. We start small–"

Isaac's voice bordered on hysteria. "Peter!"

"–only the basics. The rest will come later, although–"

"Do we have to face him?" Now Gen's voice quivered just the same.

"Enough!" Peter shouted. "Fear and power. These are the only two elements I will forbid you to mingle with. I will not have your minds corrupted. You will learn what you need to learn, and you will act in the ways in which you must. The rest will come naturally, far more smoothly if you resist the urges you currently seem to be succumbing to."

Silence crowded the room for a number of moments.

"So, the basics. Are you ready to learn?"

I couldn't speak over the sound of blood rushing through my ears, so I merely nodded.

I was reminded of hide and seek. Smelling the Dawn detergent lingering on the towels of the linen closet I always chose to hide in, hearing my dad's voice counting down through the peeling door, almost taunting as it reached the last few numbers. Then, finally... *Ready or not, here I come.*

I would clench my hands, ball them into fists to keep them from shaking. This is what I did as Peter stood and led us away from the kitchen, even as my heart continued to pound.

I glanced at Gen anxiously. *Home,* I mouthed.

"Gen," I hissed once Peter was out of earshot. "We need to ask him about going home."

"It didn't feel natural!"

"This isn't like saying 'I love you' too soon, Gen! It's important!"

"We'll get to it," she said. She grabbed my hand and wrapped her pinky around mine. "I promise."

She released my hand and followed Peter. I hung back, sighed deeply, then followed her. "Okay," I muttered. "Okay."

As soon as Peter stopped walking, I spoke. "We need to know that we can get home."

"Sorry?"

"You heard her," Gen said, suddenly confident. "We need an insurance policy. If we want to go home, you need to let us."

Peter paused in his walking for a moment. "No."

"No?" Gen's voice hit a high note.

"Well, in a sense, no. I need to ensure that you won't simply panic and be gone. You know what I've brought you here for–"

I bit back the response that we didn't, not really anyways.

"–and that is enough to know the stakes. I will still give you a portion of insurance, however. Tomorrow morning. I'll give you three some time to talk before we resume our learning, and you can decide what you truly desire. To stay, or to go. I am sorry to say I cannot be any more liberal in my policy. Losing you in a fit of fancy is far too great a fear of mine."

The three of us met eyes. Gen sighed deeply. "Alright. Tomorrow morning, then."

Peter smiled, and this time it carried none of the artifice of before. "Perfect. Oh, and don't worry about your parents. I can send you back to the exact moment you left. To the exact second, if I do it right."

The work was tedious. When Peter said the basics, he truly meant it. My hands fumbled with the tiny screwdrivers, constantly sliding from their assigned seats within the divots of the screws. I was attempting to remove the face from one of the watches from the display cases in the front of the store, trying to slip in the question of home.

"Customer stock," Peter had called the watches. "No powers, beyond, of course, the knowledge of the time of day."

When I finally managed to get the face off, Peter walked us through the gears, slowly pointing to each one and explaining its connections.

By the end of the day, my fingers burned and my eyes were sore from squinting. Gen's were as wide as ever, but Isaac's drooped, just as exhausted as mine. Peter began leading us back to our rooms.

"When you wake," he said as he walked, "you'll find I've provided some clothes in your rooms. Feel free to try them on. After all," – he gestured to our jeans and t-shirts – "it isn't 2018 anymore."

I suppressed a laugh at just how true that was.

# CHAPTER FOUR

"Oh my god. I *can not* wear one of these."

Gen and I gazed into the wardrobe in the room Peter had lead us to the previous night, and we were met with some of the frilliest dresses we had ever seen.

"I don't think we have much of a choice," Gen grimaced, "and, oh," she teased, "Don't forget your corset… and your petticoats… and your stockings… and your-"

"I get it, I get it!" I groaned and pulled a pale blue dress with minimal frill off of the hanger.

"Excellent choice, Cinderella," Gen mocked, as she selected a pale green style hanging a few away from my selection.

"Hey," I teased, "I'll take Cinderella. Either way, you shouldn't get too cocky. *You're* going to have to take out the ponytail you always insist on!"

"Ugh," Gen moaned, tugging at the elastic band constantly holding back her dark frizzy curls, "Don't remind me."

I tossed my hair over one broad shoulder, I trying to reach around and tie the strings of the corset I had pulled on, but my flexibility failed me. I groaned. "Can you lace my corset?"

The room appeared to be something straight out of a fairytale, a notion that made my childhood heart sing. The bed and wardrobe were both made of a rust-colored wood with intricately carved flowers etched deep into the boards. The grey stone walls were speckled with oil lamps resting upon ornate copper bases, interrupted by a draping tapestry depicting a bumblebee meandering throughout a field of poppies. The room held the grandeur of a castle, the very air laced with magic and wonder.

"So what do you think Peter meant?" Gen said from behind me.

"About wha- *Ow!*" I was interrupted by a little gasp when she drew the lace of my corset tighter. "That's unpleasant. Speaking of which, why did you kick me earlier? When we were talking to Peter, I mean."

"Sorry, I just didn't want you to make Peter mad before we found out everything." Gen gave a final tug on my laces to make sure the knot would hold. "Okay, you're done, now do mine."

We traded off places, then I began on the lace of her corset, and she continued.

"Anyways, you know what I meant. About teaching us how to control time! I thought being a doctor would be cool!"

"First of all," I teased, grabbing Gen by the shoulders and turning her to face me, "you're a nerd." Gen snickered. "Second, yeah, this is crazy. I mean, part of me is all for this stuff, you know, carpe every diem, but then..." I trailed off for a second, chewing on my lip. "Part of me kind of just wants to go back to Gillonsville." She shot me a look. "*Our* Gillonsville," I admonished.

"Kels." Gen was looking me dead in the eye, which confused me for a minute, until I realized she was kneeling on the bed to be at eye level with me. "Nerd is not an insult."

I laughed. "That's what you felt the need to say so seriously?"

"It's more of an aside. My point is it's *way* too early to be having doubts. Peter controls time, so he can probably send us back to the exact moment we left and we won't have missed a thing. And he said staying was our choice. But this is our "Yer a wizard, Harry" moment!" She paused, eyes flashing wildly as she jumped up off the bed. "Are you really telling me that you'd rather be a muggle?"

I glanced in the mirror to check my ensemble. "But what about 'him.'" I drew air-quotes around the word. "The rouge apprentice, I mean. Aren't you worried about that?"

"Kelsey. This is an adventure! If we want to be the protagonists, we have to have an antagonist."

I snorted. "I'll say it again: You're a nerd."

"That doesn't change the fact I'm right."

I paused for a moment. Was I too much in my head here? I always complained that in Gillonsville everything was predictable. Well, there was certainly no predicting what would happen to us here. In the mirror my fists bunched the blue silk of my skirt. I quickly let go and smoothed the fabric back into place. "Hermione never had to wear a corset," I muttered to my reflection.

"Hermione would have sucked it up and gotten on with it," Gen called over her shoulder. "Now come on. I can't wait to see Isaac."

"Man, I hope he's wearing pantaloons."

I pushed the door open and stepped out into the hallway, clapping my hand over my mouth as it became clear Gen's hope had been fulfilled.

"Well, you certainly look... *Gentlemanly*." Gen's comment came through a muffled snort.

Isaac put up a hand in resignation. He was dressed in plaid pantaloons, a white button down with puffy sleeves, a light brown vest, and a crimson scarf tied in a reluctant bow around his neck.

"I know right," he lamented, "I look like Bach, or something."

"No," I corrected. "You look like an idiot."

At this, he deepened his voice and with an abysmal German accent quoted,"If I decide to be an idiot, then I'll be an idiot on my own accord."

"How am *I* the nerd if you casually quote Bach?" Gen asked.

"It's interesting!" Isaac protested.

" Math is interesting!" Gen fired back.

"Speaking of interesting," I interjected, "where's Peter?"

"Well, he said he was going to give us a little bit of time to decide what we wanted to do, remember?" Isaac reasoned.

"My mind's made up," Gen said firmly. "I want to stay. This is a once in a lifetime opportunity, and I want to take it." She scanned our faces expectantly, and I shifted my footing.

"I still don't know, Gen," I said, wincing only slightly when she pressed her mouth into a slight pout. "It's just the whole rogue apprentice thing. I mean, how on earth are we supposed to handle that. We're just… Well, honestly, we're just us."

"But that's the whole point!" Gen exclaimed. "We're *us*. Right now, being us doesn't mean anything. I want it to. What do you think, Isaac?"

Just as he opened his mouth to speak, the unmistakable sound of shattering glass rippled through the hallway.

"Peter?" Gen shouted. I could hear her breathing speeding up.

We stood in silence for a moment. Then, suddenly, there was a reply that made my heart sink all the way to my shoes. A scream.

"Peter!" Gen yelled again, taking off at a sprint in the direction of the scream. "Peter!"

Isaac and I took off after her.

I could barely hear our footsteps over the sound of my thoughts thundering through my brain. *This was a bad idea. We should have gone home when we had the chance and now we're going to be stuck and Peter's gone and we still don't know who he is and... and...*

"Uh, guys." Gen's voice was small, a trait I had never associated with her. Gen was vibrant, strong. Gen didn't hesitate. "You might want to come see this."

I followed her voice, and rounded the corner into a room at the end of the hallway.

"I'm sure there's no reason to be worried." Isaac's attempts at levity fell flat.

"No reason to be worried? Isaac, are your glasses broken? Look!"

I followed the slant of Gen's arm, choking on my breath as I saw what lay beneath. A watch –not just a watch, Peter's watch– shattered on the ground. The face lay in a halo of crystalline shards, the metal frame bent and warped as though it were made of nothing stronger than aluminum foil. The gears were at a standstill, a distant relative of the churning and tumbling cogs we had seen only one day earlier.

"Okay, okay, let's be logical about this." I could hear in Gen's tone that she was struggling for mental footing. She tapped her foot. "Logical, logical. Maybe he's still here?"

I looked back down at the watch. "I don't mean to be pessimistic, but I feel like that's pretty unlikely."

"How would you know?" Gen didn't sound angry, although she might have to any passerby. I knew her well enough to know what it really was: fear.

"Well, he seemed pretty nervous about keeping any watches with power out of the wrong hands. Naturally, his would have that power. There's no way he would have given it up unless someone took it from him."

Isaac bit his lip. "So, is there someone in the building?"

"No," Gen whispered. "No. There couldn't be."

"Are you sure?" Isaac's panic was palpable.

"I had to open the door."

He stepped forward. "What?"

"When I came into the room, the door was closed. I had to open it. If someone took Peter out of the room in a hurry, they would have left the door open."

I felt my stomach twist violently, and I rubbed my sweaty palms on the light blue fabric of my dress. "Are you saying what I think you are?"

"There's no other way..."

The final phrase came in unison. "He time travelled."

Isaac spoke first. "Where do we even start?"

We were back in the kitchen, hunched over the thick wooden table. Although Gen and Isaac both looked calm, I had a feeling they were acting similarly to me, building dams to hold our fear in a place where it couldn't cloud our reasoning.

"Well, I think it's clear that we have two tasks," Gen said matter-of-factly.

"Enlighten us," Isaac replied.

"It's pretty obvious, really. First, we have to figure out how to use the watches ourselves. If Peter time travelled, odds are we can't get to him just through being here."

"Unless someone just used it to get him out of the room, then brought him back to this year in a different location," Isaac pointed out.

"That's a real possibility," Gen said, "which leads me to our second task. Finding leads on Peter."

"It's pretty clear who took him," I said softly. "It has to be the rogue apprentice, right?"

"Most likely," Gen affirmed. "But that could be anyone. Peter was too vague for us to really know. So we need to figure out who that was. My hope is that Peter has a journal we can look through, something that might have more of an identifier."

My cheeks turned slightly pink as I imagined reading his journal. Although it was clearly necessary, it felt like such an intrusion. I quashed the feeling, reminding myself that he would have no way of knowing one way or the other.

"I think the watches are the bigger job," Gen continued, "so we should have two people on that. I'm thinking me and Isaac. You need to look for the leads, Kelsey."

"Why?"

Isaac butted in before Gen could answer. "It's right up your alley, Kels. You can read people way better than me and Gen. Plus, Gen needs someone to boss around, and I need someone to boss me around."

Gen stuck her tongue out at Isaac, suddenly looking five years younger than her thirteen normally afforded.

I sucked in a deep breath through clenched teeth. "Okay. Okay. I can do it."

Gen broke out into a broad grin. "Yeah, you can."

# CHAPTER FIVE

A few moments later I found myself back in the stone-floored hallways of the watchmaker's. My chest felt tight. It reminded me of pulling back a rubber band, and waiting for the cold sting of when it snapped back.

I liked to consider myself the kind of person who was able to manage stress. Calm, cool, and collected. But that was never me, and in that moment I felt it more than ever.

Peter was gone.

I was fearful for obvious reasons, obvious reasons which my mind assaulted me with the memory of at a painfully rapid pace. We didn't know what we were doing. Peter had barely taught us anything. We didn't know how to construct even the most basic watches, never minding the matter of those with the capabilities of time travel.

But it wasn't just that, although it probably should have been. More pressing in my mind was the feeling of having lost our choice. With Peter still here, we had the chance to back out, the chance to decide if we were really equipped to handle the things which he intended us to. Now, we had no choice. It didn't matter if we were ready, or even if we could be ready.

I could hear Gen's voice in my head, a constant foil to my self doubt, but it didn't seem to matter.

As I rounded the corner into Peter's bedroom, I felt as though I was falling. I was reminded of a trip my family went on when I was ten years old to the Columbia River Gorge, where a thick train of water broke apart the Oregon-Washington border. The hike was near a waterfall, and about halfway through the trek, we reached a plunging slope of pebbles, washed slick with runoff from the falls. My father had already made it to the bottom, and was waiting with outstretched arms. "Don't worry, Kelsey," he said. "Just take it slow. You won't fall."

I placed a hesitant toe of my purple Sketchers on to the first stone, and exhaled. *Easy.* The second foot followed. Still, no problem. My doubt began to subside before slowly, then all at once, I began to slide. My arms windmilled beside me as I slid down the rocks, fighting for traction on the slippery stones. It seemed as though I fell forever.

This was how I felt. I felt as though I was ten years old, screaming down a hill, praying that I could catch myself before I crashed.

I tried to steal myself as I took in the sights of Peter's room for the second time. Gen had scraped the broken pieces of the watch off of the floor previously, so it looked as though Peter could have walked back in at any moment, straightened the sheets on his bed, and launched into another one of his lessons. *Snooping around, are you Kelsey? Don't worry, there's nothing in here you won't learn eventually.* He would place a knotted hand against my back and gently guide me out of the room. *But not yet. These things are not for you, not until I decide they are.*

Peter hadn't been gone for that long, but already the loss stung. I didn't know him well, obviously, but his sudden trust in us, and our sudden trust in him –however forced– had made it seem so. His loss was an empty space in my chest, filled with a substance that both cooled and burned.

I looked around the room, forcing myself to focus. I walked the few yards to his bed, and straightened the sheets as I considered where he may have stashed a journal. A bookshelf stood diagonal from the bed, and I stepped toward it.

There were maroon books with ribbed spines, deep purple books with gold-lettered titles, dark turquoise books with silver etching, anything and everything.

There were both unmarked volumes, dogeared with creased spines and surprisingly familiar works, the likes of Romeo and Juliet, Gulliver's Travels, and the Odyssey.

I let my hand brush along the shelves, displacing the fine layer of dust that had gathered on the surface of the wood.

Almost three-quarters of the way across, I paused, noticing a slim break in the constant shadow of gray the dust had been providing.

My eyes traced the line of negative space and instantly saw the origins of the break. The book which had been there, if the other packed-to-the-brim shelves were anything to go by, was missing. I scanned the room, looking for any other sign of the missing volume along the dusky interior.

On the other side of the bed, Peter had stashed a simple desk, carved of what looked to be mahogany. It had a few drawers, all of which were fitted with bronze handles. Beside it, a book lay face open on the ground. I walked over and picked it up, leaving my finger in the page it had been open to.

The leather volume appeared to be a journal, with pages clearly not from it crammed within its own, giving it an overstuffed appearance. The spine was slim but sturdy, unmistakably the missing volume.

The journal's pores seeped what felt to me to be an essence of Peter, distinctly him despite my short knowledge of the man.

I cracked the front cover, revealing a title page bearing the same calligraphic handwriting from both of the notes, spelling out *The Watches and Their Peculiar Habits.* Then, below it, in a slightly smaller print: *Property of Peter Q. Montague*

I shoved a piece of paper from the desk in between the page it had been opened to, then took off for the dining room.

Isaac and Gen were still there when I entered, more collapsed than seated.

"I take it no luck on your end, then?" I asked.

He laughed mirthlessly. "Does it look like it? A whole half-an-hour and we have nothing. Nothing!"

I gave a consolatory grimace.

"Don't be so dramatic, Isaac," Gen interjected. "Listen to yourself. *A half-an-hour.* This isn't exactly algebra homework. We're bound to have to work a little bit."

Isaac folded his arms and leaned back in his seat.

Gen turned to me. "How about on your end?"

"Well, guess what I've got."

"Oh my god, please tell me you found his journal," Isaac whined.

I dropped it on the table with a triumphant thud.

Isaac pumped his fist.

"So, this is it?" Gen said the statement with an air of reverence, not disappointment, eyes wide. I knew that she must have been thinking what I was, relishing the very *Peter-ness* which the book exuded.

Gen's slim fingers carefully undid the leather strap holding the book shut, and as the pressure was released it sprang open a bit, as if it had a life of its own.

We exchanged glances.

"I hadn't opened it yet," I said, looking critically at the squat book. "Well, besides the title page. *The Watches and Their Peculiar Habits.*"

Isaac tilted his head.

"I know," I said. "That's what Peter wanted to call it, I guess. I feel like we're hardly in a position to judge him."

We leafed through the other pages in quiet astonishment, making our acquaintance with the wonders the journal contained.

There were intricate diagrams, summaries of experiments, theories, just about everything else you could dream of tucked away into the home of the leather-bound book. "Where did you get all this, Peter?" I said through a breath as my fingers traced over a diagram involving stars and planets arranged into a system so tightly knit the page almost seemed to overflow with the magnitude of the ink.

After a few minutes of gawking, I pulled the book away from them. "Wait a minute. I almost forgot. When I found this, it wasn't on his desk. It was turned over on the ground, almost like it was knocked over. I stuck a note in the page it was open to."

I slid my finger into the pages, and flipped it open, letting the note fall to the table.

"I don't get it," Gen said promptly. "This seems so average. Why would he–"

I grabbed Gen's hand just as she was about to turn the page. "Gen, are you even reading this?"

I pushed her hand away and lifted the book off the table. My heart raced as I traced the words.

"Kelsey, what's wrong?" Isaac asked, scooting marginally closer to my seat.

"Are you scared?" Gen's frown deepened. "You're pale, and your palms are sweaty. I can see your lower lip starting to tremble. I haven't seen you do that since Mr. Tybalt yelled at you when he saw–"

"Gen, stop it. Just read." I shoved the book toward her and gulped hard. Peter had mentioned a rogue apprentice, but I had never expected... Isaac whispered the words of the entry out loud as he read them.

> *"August 15th. He came back today. Erindale, I mean. It had been several months, and I won't pretend that a sour taste didn't flood my mouth when I saw him. I knew why he had come, he'd threatened it before. But nevertheless, I began to show him the watches, just like I would any other customer. I figured, however stupidly, that perhaps he would back off if I didn't show any signs of distress, but before I could even discuss one model he kicked one of my legs out from under me. He just kept repeating the same few words as I lay there. "Show me. Show me. You'd never tell me before but I'm stronger now. Show me." Naturally, at first, I feigned confusion. Told him I didn't know what he meant. The folly of an old man, I suppose, figuring my simple act would be enough to deter him. But he was having none of it. He was insistent, asking and asking. "I was your apprentice," he insisted. "You were supposed to trust me, you had to trust me." I told him nothing, still. He said he'd be back. He said that next time he'd come for more than just the purple-"*

He let his voice drop. "That's it. Weird that he'd stop in the middle of a sentence."

Gen turned to Isaac slowly, now trembling in the same way I had been. "Don't you get it, Isaac? It's torn out. It was knocked over, and there's a page torn out. Someone took it. *Erindale* took it."

"He's the rogue apprentice," I whispered.

"And *he* has Peter."

All the blood rushed out of Isaac's face, and had he not been sitting down I would have feared he was at risk of passing out.

I took the journal back from Gen, running a finger in between the two missing pages, my fingers meeting a jagged edge. "He took it in a hurry." I could hear my voice. I was terrified. Why did it sound so dull?

"Erindale…" Gen repeated, ignoring my remark.

"Does it sound familiar?" Isaac asked.

She shook her head. "Should it?"

"Not in any context I can think of."

"How can we find him?" I said.

"We can't," Isaac said quickly, voice jumping almost a full octave. "It's not safe, we're not ready, and even if we were we wouldn't even know where to start, and even if we did…"

"Isaac," Gen said, as calmly as she could seem to muster. "We're never going to be ready if you go and hyperventilate on us. Now is the time to figure out how we're going to find him."

His eyes grew wider.

Gen sighed. "Look, it doesn't exactly sound great to me either, but we have no other option. The only logical reason someone would take the time to steal the entry would be if it was about them."

"I don't get it," I said, bunching the fabric of my dress in my hands. "Why not just take the whole journal. It would have been faster, never mind not left us with any sort of lead."

Isaac blinked rapidly. "You don't think... You don't think he *wants* us to find him, do you?"

"Don't be ridiculous," Gen countered. "If he wanted us to find him he would have left a note. There has to be some other explanation."

"Which is? Not to be the devil's advocate here, Gen, but Isaac is right. There's no other reason he wouldn't take the whole thing."

"Well, that shouldn't stop us," Gen said firmly. "We still have to find Peter. Look. He said he needed us. I don't intend to let him down just because we're afraid that this "Erindale" person might be luring us in."

My fear had weight in my stomach. I could feel it sitting there, a lump deep in my gut both the size and shape of a peach pit.

"Ok, so we find him," Isaac agreed tentatively. "But somehow I doubt 'yellowpages.com' has been invented yet."

"Yeah, but you know," I retorted, pushing aside my fear, "we could use the *actual yellow pages.*"

Joking. I could do that. I needed to, at least for now. Float the fear away, but tether it so you can pull it back later.

"Actually–" Gen cut into our argument. "Both of you are wrong. Even the *'actual yellow pages'* weren't invented for at least," she glanced down at her watch, "75 years give or take."

"Ok, then riddle me this," Isaac returned Gen's pointed intelligence without missing a beat, "What exactly *should* we use?"

"The journal, of course," Gen said, looking remarkably clear-eyed. "It seems to be a bit of a tell-all– excluding the ripped up parts, of course. There's no reason our plan needs to change. Regardless of what happens, we still need to know how to use the watches. So, Kelsey keeps reading the journal, and we keep going on the mechanics. It's not complicated." She said the last bit of her monologue blankly.

I admired how she managed to sustain her certainty. I had never felt the kind of unabashed confidence Gen displayed on a more than regular basis. But yet, there she was, dishing out orders. A proper leader. For whatever reason, that thought hit a sore spot.

I'd never been one to lead. Gen had always been the front runner, ever since we all met, assigned to the same group project about the water cycle in our third grade gifted and talented class. Her voice then had been babyish, stumbling over words with too many syllables for her smaller tongue. But even then, she was a sargent, delegating pieces of the poster we had been instructed to make to each of us.

"Isaac." I could hear that voice in my head, even five years later. "You have the best handwriting, so you should do the lettering."

Isaac beamed. Gen turned to me, her small face scrunching up as she looked me up and down. "You're quiet," she had said. She was nothing if not blunt, even then. "What do you do?"

"I-I don't know. Not much, r-really." I had stuttered slightly in my younger years.

She smiled. Her smile hadn't changed. "Now I'm sure that's not true. Here," she said, shoving the iPad the teacher had given us in my direction. "I'll start drawing. You research. Figure out how rain works."

My smile that day had almost broken my face in two. Nobody had ever trusted me the way Gen did, the way Gen does still. So maybe I couldn't lead, but I was trusted. That would have to be enough.

I managed to completely tune out Gen and Isaac as I worked, pouring over Peter's handwriting. At some point, Gen had slipped me some paper and a pen, where I now took messy notes in scrawling black ink. *Started the business himself,* was at the top of the list, a revelation from the first entry. Further down: *Does he have a son?* Which I had later crossed out and replaced with, *No biological son.* Finally I crossed out son, and replaced it with *family.*

I had a sudden thought. Maybe… I stuck the note back into the page I was on, and flipped to the very back of the journal.

"Bingo," I whispered. Gen and Isaac were already looking up when I met their gaze.

"What is it?" Isaac said, hope barely restrained to the edges of his voice.

I pointed to the open page, gesturing for Gen and Isaac to read.

Isaac smirked. "The yellow pages," he said proudly. "Way to go, Kels." He pulled the journal in front of him.

In the back of his journal, Peter had sequestered a list of names and locations, all alphabetized. He'd left blank space under the bottom of the sections for each letter. The Z's had almost a full page of blank space, only one name at the top. The S's, on the other hand, were cramped, extra names squeezed into the margins, packed like commuters into a too-busy subway car.

I indicated to Isaac to pause in his turning.

I looked more closely at the list. Below every city name was a third line, preceded by a y which was followed by a four digit number. "Wait a minute. Does that mean year?"

I bit my lip hard, nervousness setting in as grabbed the book back, thumbing through the alphabet until I came to rest on the Es.

"Talk about out of the frying pan and into the fire," Isaac said.

Gen stared at the paper, almost furiously, as if she was willing the words to change, presenting some alternate scenario. Eventually, I could see her glare falter. "I'll say."

For in Peter's distinctive script-like handwriting, there was not one Erindale, but two. One of which was half a century away.

*Franklin Erindale*
*Gillonsville, Connecticut*
*Y: 1811*
*Rupert Erindale*
*Gillonsville, Connecticut*
*Y: 1952*

That night – after deciding a much needed rest was worthy of a slight delay– Gen and I lay sprawled out beside each other in the bedroom. It seemed like an entirely different place from the last time we were there. Last time, it was laughter and corsets. Last time, it was pure adventure without the shadow of fear clouding all of the bright spots of opportunity.

Despite there being no light source I could find in the room, spindly shadows still danced across the ceiling.

There was a whole new symphony of sounds in this version of Gillonsville, the hum of the odd passing car engine replaced with the occasional clap of hooves on cobblestone, the sound of the neighbor's TV playing American Idol just a bit too loudly replaced with the sound of a group of men venturing home from town.

The sounds of my friends, however, were unfailingly familiar. I could hear Gen's even breaths right beside me, and despite the thick stone walls, I could hear Isaac snoring in the next room over. I hummed a sigh before turning my head on the pillow.

"Gen? You awake?"

There was a beat of silence, then the response came.

"Yeah," Gen paused and the sound of her yawn drifted through the air. "What's up?"

"Not sure," my voice was thick with sleep yet to come. "God, could he snore any louder?"

Gen laughed breathily. "Don't test him."

The conversation was familiar too, from many nights of sleepovers with Isaac in the next room over.

Another beat of silence.

"Why do you think Peter called us here? I know he gave his version of an answer, but I never got a chance to ask you what you thought he meant." My question was without prompting, but the thought had been plaguing my mind for a while.

"Hard to say, exactly. A part of me almost thinks he knew this would happen. An angry part," she added. I could sense her thought in the silence. "That entry was from August. It's October, and in the entry Peter said Erindale threatened to come back. Peter might have known Erindale would take him. But something tells me this didn't go to Peter's plan."

I rolled over. "What do you mean?"

"Well, I don't think he'd throw us in blind like this. I think he miscalculated. Thought he had more time.

Enough time to make sure we knew enough to save him. Or ourselves." Gen stopped and yawned, this time more forcefully than before. "I don't know how to feel. I'm mad, a little, at least I think. But somehow, I understand."

"Understand what?"

Gen rolled over, facing away from me. "Peter must have been scared too."

Without even saying goodnight, Gen curled up on her side of the bed, drawing her knees up to her chest.

I twisted onto my side and pressed my head into the pillow, half-smothering, half seeking-comfort.

There were shadows dancing on the wall, too.

I still couldn't find the light source.

# CHAPTER SIX

"So obviously we'll start with Franklin." Gen was remarkably awake, a trait which I had yet to match.

It was the next day, and I was leaning over the table, my hair wrestled into a messy bun, which proved a harsh contrast to the period clothing I had forced myself back into. Three empty coffee mugs and a half a loaf of bread served as our centerpiece.

"How easy do you think that's going to be?" Isaac said through a yawn, straightening his shirt absently. "Do you expect him to just be sitting on his porch in an adirondack chair sipping a glass of sweet iced tea?"

"An adirondack is the last thing I expect. We're in Connecticut not the southernmost tip of Alabama." Gen jabbed at the map of Gillonsville I had found folded in the journal, evidently handmade by Peter.

After almost a full hour of poring over the cramped handwriting and the confusingly scaled drawings and labels, I came to the conclusion cartography was clearly not a priority in the seemingly scholarly watchmaker's mind. I didn't blame him for his lack of proficiency. If I discovered something like time travel I wouldn't find much merit in learning other crafts either.

Gen and Isaac had made a latter return trip to Peter's bedroom, salvaging a large quantity of books from the shelves. Now, all the volumes they had managed to procure lay strewn open all around the map.

"How on earth are we going to do this?" Isaac said through a mouthful of one of the sandwiches we had been able to create out of the limited items in the pantry. Breakfast had gained a broader definition. He brushed a few crumbs off of his vest. He was wearing a new one today, this one a rather abysmal paisley print.

"You're going to need to be a little more specific," I said dryly.

"I wish I knew how I could be." He paused. "Let's see, specificity… Definition of 'this,'" he gestured to the books. "This: The insane conglomeration of a kidnapping, a potential need for time travel, a mysterious last name, and a lack of instruction of how to handle any of those things."

"I can't deduct any points for your eloquence," I began, "and while time travel could be a problem, it is not a problem we have now, it is a problem we have later. For now, we just have to find Franklin's address."

Gen took a bite of her sandwich and chewed thoughtfully. "It's got to be in one of these books somewhere." She grabbed the nearest book, flipped it open, and leaned in close to the text, personifying the old adage of having one's nose stuck in a book.

Isaac peered over her shoulder, and I moved to join him as I saw a look of amusement edge its way onto his face. "Hey, uh, Gen?"

"What's up?" She didn't make any move to suggest she was any less engrossed in the text, and her tone remained decidedly brusque.

"Do you consider it likely you'll find the address of a John Doe in 1811 by reading the Odyssey?"

"Is this…" She looked down at the book then placed her head down on its pages defeatedly. "I wish I could say I noticed. I'll, uh, look somewhere else."

Isaac stifled a laugh.

"You do that," I replied, setting aside the journal I had instinctually pulled towards me. "I'll head into the store. I'm not getting any closer to a real address in this journal, but I'm thinking that Peter might have kept some sort of customer log."

I was feeling more confident that day. I wouldn't necessarily call it optimism, but it was something akin to that.

Isaac spoke as he began to put away the bread. "But Erindale was an apprentice, not a customer. Why would he be in the log?"

Before I could speak, Gen interjected. "No, no, Kelsey is on to something. Peter didn't just pull Erindale out of thin air. They had to have met somehow, and there's no reason that couldn't have been through a deal."

I walked over to the pantry. "A deal gone sour."

Isaac laughed. "Not unlike this milk." He tossed me the jug. "It smells like that uber-pretentious cheese my parents like."

"You should let them know their artisan creamery actually gave them a block of toxic milk. I swear, when I saw it on your counter I was just about ready to call Area 51. The mold looked *way* too much like eyes. I had to act fast before it became sentient."

"*Trust me*," Isaac said over Gen's protest that "Cheese could not sustain sentience." "I know."

As I squatted behind the desk in the storefront it was hard to not feel slightly paranoid. The faces of the watches lining the cases felt like human faces, watching my every move. Despite my lack of familiarity with the man, I couldn't help but wonder whether or not Peter would condone my actions.

I pulled open the first drawer and tried not to feel guilty.

The drawer was almost empty, the lone occupants being a matchbox and a pipe. I mentally chided Peter, but closed the drawer nevertheless. The next two drawers were equally unexciting, one containing a leather wallet of tools, and one containing a wide array of ink and pens.

In the fourth drawer, however, I found a dusty stack of papers crudely sewn together with butcher string. I was about to pass it off as some sort of avant-garde-DIY-project-gone-rogue before I saw the letters inscribed on the front, made almost illegible with both time and a thin layer of dust.

It was unmistakably the customer log, although it seemed strangely archaic relative to Peter's other possessions. I opened it to the first page, and was met with an explosion of dust which burned my lungs.

When my eyes stopped watering I skimmed a few lines of the spreadsheet-like text. As one typically does when presented with a list of stranger's names, my mind began to wander as I began to think about who they could be.

Who was Eileen Flanagan, and what compelled her to buy a watch which, according to Peter's description was "silver with a black face." Was it a gift for her husband? Her father? Was she a teacher? Did she have children? The foggy image presenting itself to me featured a woman who was too old to be considered young, but too young to be considered middle aged. She had red wavy hair, and although her rather robust nature wouldn't suggest it, she could play the piano as if her fingers were calling down angels.

However, and this is the very magic of inventing stories for strangers, it was equally probable she was none of those things. Maybe she was a petite blonde who only spoke when spoken to, but had a mind to rival the one of Albert Einstein.

The lists went on and on, and I was on about the fifth page of Carl Lexingtons and Jeremy Sagats before I noticed my back beginning to protest my hunched over stance on the stone floor.

I stretched, then closed the log, making sure to turn away slightly as I did so as to avoid any more dust related mishaps.

"You are *not* an 'avid researcher,' Isaac!" Gen was saying. "Plus, even if I were to agree you research more than me it would only be because of your geeky obsession with-"

She broke off as she became aware of my laughing. I felt, for the first time since the ordeal had begun, a sense of relief. Things were as normal as they could have been given the circumstances, and my gratitude was tangible.

"Sorry to interrupt," I said, walking over the table from my position in the doorway. "I take it by your arguing you got *loads* done."

"For sure," Isaac said blankly. "In fact, we've found him already. And while we were at it, we discovered the meaning of life too."

"Glad to hear it. Enlighten me." I sat down across from Isaac.

"You've cornered me Kels. I suppose I'll have to reveal the secret. The meaning of life is…"

"Stop wasting time," Gen said, eyeing the log. "Is that what I think it is?"

"Yep. One logbook dating all the way back to 1800-"

"Which would be a lot more impressive if 1800 wasn't technically eleven years ago."

"Why so cynical?" Isaac cut in.

"I'm not cynical, I'm a realist," Gen reasoned. "You realize in modern time that's the equivalent of something from 2007. *We* are older than that book."

"Okay, both of you need to dial it back a bit. It doesn't matter how old it is. It matters if it's useful."

Gen huffed the beginning of a retort, but then dwindled off before any comprehensible words got out. "Okay, okay, you're right," she said, shifting forward in her seat. "So Franklin, 1811. He'd be towards the end, then." She began flipping pages.

"If he was even a customer," Isaac muttered.

I couldn't keep in a sigh. "Even a *tiny* bit of optimism would be excellent right now, Isaac."

"Just saying!"

"Well, what is it you were 'just saying?'" Gen said, her finger planted in the middle of a page of the log. "Because I just found him. Franklin Erindale. Pocket watch. Silver chain, silver face, white detailing."

My excitement was coupled with confusion. "Pocket watch? How's that supposed to work?"

Gen shrugged. "No idea. But it's not worth missing out on the opportunity just because we aren't sure of one detail."

"Is it really just one detail though?" Isaac said, leaning over to read the paper. "The only thing we truly fundamentally know about the watches is they work when we put them on our wrists. Pocket watches take wrists entirely out of the equation."

"Yeah," Gen reasoned, "but if he was an apprentice, he knew what he was doing. We have no clue how the watches work. There's no obvious reason for it to require the physical act of placing a watch on one's wrist."

"Gen's right," I said, before Isaac had a chance to rebuke. "We can't really afford to leave any door closed." As I spoke I noticed the corner of the page was partially folded over. Gently, I took the book from Gen, peeled the page back, and smiled. "And it looks like we won't have to."

# CHAPTER SEVEN

I felt as if there was something I needed to do to get ready, although I was already fully clothed in the blue dress. My anticipation was in a way eager, but with an equal measure of nervousness. I could feel the same emotions in the atmosphere of the kitchen, radiating in slow waves off of Isaac and Gen. It had been about an hour since we had found the address in that folded over corner, but yet we were all still there. I knew the reason, although I also knew none of us would admit it.

I caught my reflection in the back of a spoon, and I stared for a moment. The girl who I saw looking back at me was barely someone I knew. In fifth grade history class, we learned that rather than using blush, ladies in the seventeenth century would pinch their cheeks, creating the illusion of pinker cheeks. I needed to do no such thing, as I could already see a substantial flush making its way across my nose and cheeks. I looked away.

I twisted the fabric of the dress into a ball then released it, smoothing it out. Twist, release, smooth. Twist, release, smooth. The pattern began to feel so natural that I lost track of the fact I was doing it. I didn't really feel as fearful as the repetitive rhythm would suggest, but my hands continued with a mind entirely their own.

"Hold on. What's our cover? Three unaccompanied thirteen-year-olds in 1811 is hardly a common sight." Gen's voice broke in, and the rhythm stopped.

"Schoolwork?" Isaac questioned.

"No." Gen groaned, standing and beginning to pace. "As much as I hate to say it, nobody will buy that."

Isaac cocked his head, and Gen sighed.

"Privilege," she muttered. "Isaac… Kelsey and I are both girls, and I'm Latina. We couldn't be going to school in this era."

"Okay." Isaac drummed his fingers on the kitchen table. "New plan. If someone asks… I improv."

"Improv?" I asked, looking up. "That's a pretty big promise coming from someone who has no acting experience beyond Ms. Combs' middle school acting class."

"Excuse you!" Isaac announced. "*I* am a renowned actor. Don't you remember *Grease*?"

I did. The school had put on the show the previous year, Isaac placed in the starring role of the world's nerdiest Danny Zuko. I smirked. "How could I forget?"

"See! I'm qualified. Am I not qualified?" He turned to Gen, doing his best impersonation of innocence.

"Sure, Isaac." She smiled warmly. "I'm willing to accept that plan if only so we can get out of here."

My eyes widened.

"What?" she asked. "You aren't excited? I can't wait. It's like a historical reenactment, but we're really there! What could be cooler?"

"Hey!" Isaac protested. "History's my thing. Stay with your math or science… Or whatever."

"My 'whatever' is going to change the world someday," Gen proclaimed. "But only if we figure out how to get home. Come on! Let's go already."

The walk to the front entrance of the shop was somber but not solemn, at least for me. We were silent but not sorrowful, simply hushed by the beckoning of the unfamiliar while we still half wanted to be pulled back into the familiar.

It was strange. Despite this being our second full day in 1811, we hadn't actually left the confines of the watchmaker's yet. There was an eerie sort of apprehension which came in a package deal with leaving.

I pushed open the door and stepped out onto the street.

It was raining. It rained the way it only rained in Connecticut, beckoning an all too welcome sense of home.

The droplets painted everything a slightly darker shade. The man in the light blue now sported a darker hue, the woman's red parasol was now flecked with crimson, and the gray cobblestones were speckled with little round dots of black.

Clouds coated most of the sky, turning our surroundings almost dusky despite it being only one o'clock or so, an estimate which a glance at my watch later confirmed.

"Excuse me, sir?" I almost started laughing at Isaac's language, but stopped myself. "I'm new 'round these parts, and I was wondering if you could perhaps point me in the direction of Marist Drive."

"Of course, my fine lad!" The subject of Isaac's inquiries, a man wearing a mustard colored vest and a black hat, pointed down the street. "It's just down that way."

"Thank you! Good day sir!"

"Good day to you too!" The hatted man responded, then, just as soon as he came, he was gone.

Despite it having been our plan to ask for directions, Gen, Isaac, and me being hopeless in those regards, it was striking to me how strange it felt. How separate the man's world and our worlds were. To the hatted man, we were just the average lost strangers without names. He had absolutely no clue of the insanity of our own story, and frankly if he did, he probably wouldn't believe us.

Continuing in the direction the man had pointed, I looked around at a street I had walked a million times, yet was walking for the first time.

It was a bit like meeting a celebrity. Despite them being somewhat familiar from countless hours of becoming familiar with a multitude of aspects of their character, they still feel like an entirely different person from any previous impression.

This was the closest I could get to a pinpointed feeling of how I felt in this strange permutation of the Gillonsville I knew.

Despite having the knowledge a Gillonsville like this existed, I had never necessarily felt it was real. To me, this version was real in the way a million dollars was real. I have, and likely never will, see it, and if I were to I would be practically required to face it with a certain level of skepticism.

I looked at the facades of the buildings as we walked briskly past.

Emma-Lucilla's Milliner demonstrated its presence through a blue and gray hand-painted sign hung above glass windows. The hats displayed behind the slightly smudged glass drew my mind back to the hatted man.

I was so lost in thought, to the extent I hadn't even noticed I was walking directly into the path of a man on a black horse until Isaac grabbed my arm and pulled me away.

"Watch it!"

The man on the horse had a lilting Irish accent and a vibrantly red beard to match.

"This is *too* weird," Isaac whispered, releasing me from his grip on my arm.

"That doesn't even begin to cover it," I whispered back.

"You guys talking about me?" Gen asked, leaning closer.

"Totally," I smirked. "We were talking about… What was it again, Isaac?"

Isaac grinned. "Oh, yes, we were honestly just trying to form a thought about why on earth you would wear *those* shoes with *that* dress."

"Exactly," I chimed in. "I mean, seriously Gen, heeled boots? S*o* 1800. This is 1811. Get with the program."

"You are *so* weird," Gen teased, "Though, if we're going to talk about fashion sense, aren't we going to mention Isaac's plaid *pantaloons*?" She said the last word with force.

"In case you're forgetting," Isaac protested. "We already did. From here on out I am implementing a very strict 'No talking about the pantaloons' rule."

"And you will be enforcing it how? You're right Gen. I mean, what a statement."

"Silence peasants!" Isaac held up his hand, "Breaking this rule is punishable by getting stabbed in the neck."

Gen rolled her eyes. "Whatever. Anyways, I hate to sound like one of Isaac's brothers, but *are we there yet*?"

I looked around, then down at the scrap of paper I had copied the address onto. "No idea," I said, squinting down the road. "Maybe."

"Kels, it being 1811 doesn't change the fact it's still our city. Let me see the paper."

I resigned it to Isaac. He copied my squint. "Uh, left at the next intersection."

Gen laughed, and reached out. "Maybe it would be a left, if you weren't holding the map upside-down." She reached over and turned it in his hands. "*Right* at the next intersection."

"This is ridiculous." Isaac announced. "Anyways, in this rain we're going to come to Franklin's looking like we've been through a tsunami."

"Anything else, Negative-Nancy?" Gen said. "Also, put the paper in your vest unless you never want to be able to read the address again."

Isaac shoved the paper into his vest petulantly. "I'm not going to tell you you're right."

"I didn't expect you to," Gen said, smiling. "And I don't need you to. Kelsey knows I'm right."

"Hey! Leave me out of this!"

"But you know I am!"

Our conversation carried us as much as our feet, and eventually we reached 5 Park Farm Lane. By then we were hopelessly drenched, but our spirits were high enough for it to not really seem to matter.

"Are you ready for this?" I said, starting across the muddy grass towards the door.

Gen half-laughed. "Does it matter?"

Before I could answer Isaac was knocking on the door, and I instantly felt compelled to make at least some sort of effort to fix my rain soaked half ponytail. My fingers were halfway through a section of my hair when the knob turned.

A small window in the center of the door slid aside, and I held my breath.

Two amber eyes peered through the window, scanning our faces carefully. Then, the window was closed again, and the eyes disappeared. The knob on the door began to twist, and it swung open about an inch. Now, the two eyes were given more form. A tall man stood in the doorway, dark hair pulled back into a low ponytail. His lips barely moved when he spoke.

"Who are you?" Although it was clearly a question, his tone remained entirely flat throughout.

Gen stepped forward. "We're looking for Franklin."

The man gave no indication that he heard her. He looked to Isaac. "Who are you?"

"*We,*" Isaac said, leaning on the word, "are looking for Franklin. As my friend already said."

The man continued to look past Gen. "Who?"

"Listen up," Isaac said, face suddenly darkening. "I don't know who you think you are but I can guarantee that Genevieve is smarter than you'll ever be, if only because she doesn't think it's okay to–"

"Walter, is there a problem?" The new voice came from behind the man. It was light, almost flowery.

"None at all, Margaret," the man yelled. *"Go away,"* he all but hissed.

"Walter, don't think I can't hear you! What did I tell you about being rude to callers. This is not your home, and although you see it as your duty to be here I assure you that it is not and that if I have a problem with your behavior I will not hesitate to kick. You. Out."

Walter was pushed away, and the door swung open far wider.

"Walter!" the woman, Margaret, said through a gasp. "Why they're only children! Why on earth would you..." She trailed off, evidently noticing Gen, who had gone uncharacteristically quiet. "Walter so help me if you were going to turn these children away because –What is your name, dear?"

"Genevieve."

"If you were going to turn them away because *Genevieve's* skin is a few hues darker than yours you may pack your bags tonight. I'm inviting them in. I expect you to have made us tea by the time we are settled in the sitting room."

I instantly felt a rush of affection for Margaret. As we entered the house, wiping our feet on the mat inside, I took Gen's hand and squeezed it. Her brown eyes met my blue, and I could see something I couldn't usually see. Something which read as... ashamed? I didn't –or, more accurately, couldn't– understand. Gen drew in a deep breath, and the look retreated. I felt my stomach turn.

A few moments later, the three of us sat on a paisley couch, situated across from Margaret, who sat in a blue wingback chair. Walter had handed us tea a few seconds after we were seated, as instructed, and now we all held steaming mugs in our shaking hands.

"So," she said finally. "What can I do for you?"

Margaret was old, but she was a beautiful kind of old, the kind which suggested she had made a deliberate effort in her childhood to avoid scrunching her eyes when she smiled. A few wrinkles crossed her face in the obligatory places, but there were none that seemed to come in excess. Her gray hair was drawn into a high bun which accentuated her cheekbones. The dress she wore hugged her slender form from the base of her neck to her hips, before jutting out into a wider stretch of fabric.

"You've already done so much, thank you," I said, trying to maintain the diplomatic air of someone from that time. "But there is one more thing, if it isn't too much trouble. Is there a Franklin that lives here?"

Her sunny face immediately went dark and I knew the answer. "Not anymore," she said, confirming what I feared. "He died last July. Scarlet Fever."

"I'm so sorry for your loss, Margar – or Ms. Erindale! Ms. Erindale." Isaac paused, blush creeping onto his cheeks..

"Margaret is just fine." She smiled without wrinkling her eyes. "It's quite alright! I'm a tough old bird. The worst part of this whole ordeal has been Walter's moving in. As my brother, he thought I was 'too fragile' to live alone after Franklin's death. How old fashioned! But yet…" She trailed off.

I smiled back. "Would you mind too terribly if we asked you some questions about your husband?"

"Not at all!" Margaret replied. Her smile grew much fuller. "I love to talk about Franklin. It makes me feel closer to him, despite… Despite everything."

"We don't want to pry…" Gen said, leaning forward.

"Oh nonsense. Please, do ask away. You had to deal with Walter. I would say that anyone deserves some hospitality after having dealt with him. But, if you don't mind me asking, who are you?"

"Well," Isaac said, a twinkle in his eye revealing his excitement. "We're all siblings." Margaret tilted her head. "Genevieve is – uh – adopted! Adopted, yes. Our Uncle Peter, he's not the most right-in-the-head, as it were. It's *very* tragic. He wandered off the other day, and we are desperately worried. At one point, he mentioned knowing a man named Franklin Erindale, so we thought that might be a good place to start."

"Oh my," Margaret said slowly.

When I spoke, it was more into my cup of tea than to her. "Did he ever mention knowing a Peter Montague?"

Her thin lips grew thinner as she pressed them together. "Montague…" she made a clicking noise with her tongue. "Not a name I remember, I'm sorry. Wait a moment… are the three of you staying alone? I hardly think that's appropriate. You must let me call on the police to–"

"No, no," Isaac said quickly, as our trio exchanged nervous glances. "I assure you that will not be at all necessary. Don't worry about us Margaret, we'll find our uncle. After all tomorrow is another day."

We were out of the door quickly after, leaving our mugs behind us.

"Well," Isaac said, shoving his hands into his pockets. "That was a dead end. Literally."

Gen snorted. "Macabre but true. But I think we're ignoring the larger point. *Gone With the Wind? Tomorrow is another day?* Really, Isaac?"

He held his hands up. "I panicked! I'd like to see you do better."

I laughed. "Alright, geek, we get it. Nicely done. But we're still stuck." I groaned, the rain still unabashedly dampening our clothes. "Just our luck. Our only lead in this century is dead."

"Look on the bright side!" Gen said.

Isaac snorted. "What bright side?"

"The tea she gave us was exceptional."

I laughed, although I wasn't sure if it was meant to be a joke. "I guess it was." Gen's capacity for unbridled optimism sometimes felt as if it could use a bridle.

"So what now?" I asked dully, kicking a pebble so it skipped across the wet stone road.

"I don't know," Gen said. At my frown, she hastily added, "but I'm sure we'll figure out something."

Isaac scoffed. "What makes you so sure?"

"The same reason we made it this far." Gen lifted up the skirt of her dress as she crossed through a puddle.

"Which is?" I looked down at my dress, the bottom three inches practically covered in mud.

"Not sure. But something got us here, and I highly doubt we lost that something just because we hit a bump in the road."

# CHAPTER EIGHT

We stumbled back through the door to the watchmakers, thoroughly soaked and exhausted. The last thing I wanted to do was keep my body upright.

"I feel like a sponge," Isaac said as we walked into the kitchen. He took of his vest and hung it on the back of a chair.

Gen kicked of her shoes. "We need to invest in a horse."

"Maybe," I said sarcastically, "but with what money?" I elected to refrain from pointing out that buying a horse would imply we planned on staying.

"Fine. We need to invest the time to *steal* a horse. Happy now?"

I laughed. "So more research? The day is still-" I checked my watch "-relatively young."

Isaac yawned. "I vote for a nap."

"A nap won't get us home," I said. "Or to Peter."

"Kelsey's right," Gen added. "You realize what Franklin being dead means, right?"

We both stared at her blankly.

"Guys... We don't have a choice anymore. We have to make it to 1952. With a task like that ahead of us, I don't think we have time for things like napping."

That settled it.

Peter's journal began to become a very familiar presence. It was somewhat relaxing to hear his voice in the pages. Although I was mostly skimming, looking for any signs of 'purple' or Erindale, I could still feel him. The comfort of this was a cork in my fear, allowing me to relax ever so slightly despite the task which lay before me.

After about an hour we had made no progress, but we had made three sandwiches.

I bit into mine, then leaned back over the journal.

"Oh my god." Gen gasped.

"Did you find something!" Isaac exclaimed excitedly.

"I wish," she said sheepishly. "This is just a good sandwich."

"Thank you for the productive dialogue," Isaac said. "However, if you could please get back to the actual matter at hand."

"Ah yes," she said, hitting the book laid open in front of her, perhaps a bit to hard. "After all, books in the 1800s are just brimming with information on time travel."

I looked away, peering back into the journal. My mouth was set in a hard line, my eyes flicking across the page steadily. I was about to give up, when suddenly I saw something which piqued my interest. An entry about Erindale dated two years prior stared back at me and I paused. "Wait a minute. I think I found something.

Isaac and I both turned to Gen, but she was so engrossed in whatever she was looking at that she didn't even seem to notice our gaze shifting to her.

"Gen!" I exclaimed.

She looked up sharply.

"I think I have something. On Erindale. Pay attention."

The authoritative tone felt unnatural coming from me, but not in a way that I particularly minded. I felt strong. Powerful, for the first time.

I jabbed my finger at a line of text.

"I think," I began slowly. "I think I might have *actually* found something."

Isaac picked up the plate with his sandwich on it and moved to peer over my shoulder, and Gen soon joined him, hands on her hips as she bent over. "What is it?"

Isaac's eager tone reminded me of the relationship between a dog towards a mailman, hopeful, but not expectant of much.

"Listen." I cleared my throat, beginning to read aloud from the journal. "*I suppose today was the day I discovered it could all go wrong. The day I realized that the world I built for myself was not an empire of steel, but rather an empire of glass. It is so unlike me, this sense of naivete I am stricken with–*"

"–Naivete?"

"It means lack of judgement. Shut up, Isaac."

"Guys. Can I continue? Good. As I was saying: *It is so unlike me–* blah, blah, blah. *I realized this transgression if only by the look in Erindale's eyes when I told him about the purple moon. Before, I had only seen in him a sort of boyish curiosity. I have to wonder if this is why I trusted him. After all, I was so similar at his age... But I digress. The truth is, in that moment, I saw not curiosity, but rather hunger. I'd never seen such a look before, but somehow, instinctually, maybe, it was recognizable. It was a desire for power. It was in this moment where I feared my apprentice's name was not Erindale, but rather Icarus. And I, Daedalus. I do hope that I am wrong."*

"Icarus?" Isaac mused. "Isn't that a Roman myth, or something?"

"Greek," Gen corrected. "In mythology, Icarus is given a pair of wings made of feathers and wax by his father. That's Daedalus. He tells Icarus to be careful, and not fly too close to the sun."

"So what's wrong?" Isaac questioned.

"He does. Icarus's ambition undoes him. He flies too close to the sun and the wings fall apart."

Isaac's tone was quiet now. "Oh."

"So the purple moon," Gen began. "Do we know what that is?"

"No," I said morosely. "I've seen it referenced a few times in the journal, but never with enough context to figure it out. Whatever it is, I can tell that Erindale wanted it pretty badly. And that Peter didn't want him to have it."

"Wait a second." Gen pulled the journal out of my hands, and turned to the still dog-eared page. "I knew it.

The first entry we read! The last word was purple. That's what it meant. The *purple* moon. So,–"

"–That's what Erindale was looking for," I finished.

"I'm almost certain of it. But what I'm not certain of is how to find it. Are you sure there was nothing in the journal?"

I shook my head slowly. "Nothing."

"Well, we have one clue."

"And what is that, Isaac?" Gen returned. Her tone was only slightly clipped.

"It's obvious, really," Isaac said, doing a perfect impression of Gen. "If Erindale wants it so badly, the 'purple moon,' or whatever it's called, must be the key to making the watches work."

"But 'purple moon…'" Gen said slowly. "It sounds more like an astrological phenomenon than an object. I'm not sure it's something we can find."

"Gen, come on," Isaac reasoned. "We saw the moon the night we came here, and you know what it distinctly was not? Purple. It's something inside of the watches, I'm almost sure of it."

"Okay," I said slowly, "So what exactly does that mean for us?"

"Well…" Gen said carefully.

"Well, what?" Isaac interjected.

"Well," Gen repeated, looking almost sympathetic, "We might have to," She paused again.

"Just spit it out!" Isaac threw up his hands, toppling the sandwich he held onto the ground.

"Ok, ok. Wow, Isaac. No need to start a food fight," Gen chastised.

I was unsure if Isaac actually heard Gen in his reassembly of his sandwich, given his lack of any reaction.

"I'm just saying we might have to cut apart one of our watches to get at the good stuff."

In her quick response to Isaac, Gen almost seemed to forget the gravity of her words, and we were left standing in reflective silence.

As my brain began to form connections and ideas, I ran into the proverbial Great Wall of China.

"Guys," I began slowly, "We *really* can't do that."

"Any other ideas?"

I could tell how stressed Gen was. Every contradiction wound her tighter and tighter.

"Gen, I'm sorry, but I think it's jumping the gun to cut apart one of the watches we already know works. If we do need to get to 1952 –and it looks like we do– we need…" I trailed off, letting the sentence fall and dissolve. "Wait…" I whispered. "We don't need to cut apart one of ours, not yet anyways. We can just take one from the storefront."

"Kelsey, that won't work," Gen said, almost incredulously. "Peter wouldn't be selling watches like that to ordinary customers. You heard him. He wouldn't even let us look at the inside of a functional one on the first day. He wouldn't just be handing them out."

"Well, ours had to come from somewhere, right? And we haven't come across any sort of workshop in the building, so odds are he made those in the storefront too. So, there have to be other functional watches stashed somewhere in the house. I just really think it's jumping the gun to cut apart one of ours."

"Kelsey…"

"Look," I said, pushing aside the journal. "I'm going to the storefront to look. You can come with me, or you can stay here. But I'm not willing to leave any stone unturned. Are you?"

I walked out of the room, and smiled as I heard annoyed muttering, followed by footsteps behind me.

When I entered the storefront, I turned hurriedly to the glass cases, squinting carefully at the watches. It was silent for a few moments before I heard Isaac and Gen enter the room.

Then, I heard a small squeak from Isaac. "Kels?"

I turned. "What's wro– Oh!" I jumped as I saw a strange man standing a few feet from the doorway.

The sight of the man wasn't particularly unnerving. He was a squat man with black tailored pants and a emerald green jacket with coattails ending just above his knees. He wore a hat which forbade me from determining the color of his hair, but I would guess it was gray, if there was anything there at all. He had an almost grandfatherly appearance, and I charted the fact he walked with a brown crooked cane as an absence of threat.

Gen gasped and Isaac's mouth hung open as if the hinge on his jaw had snapped.

"Who are you?" Isaac said, eyes gaping.

"It's not polite to gawk, young man. I expect better. My name is Harvey Abernathy. I came to–" the man paused for the briefest moment "–get my watch repaired. I bought it from Montague himself about a month back, and it has already gone positively mad. It cannot seem to keep the time no matter how many times I rewind it. I dare say it has been quite the inconvenience."

*If only he knew.*

"I'm sorry, Harvey," I replied slowly.

"Mr. Abernathy to you, young lady!" Something dark flashed through his eyes.

"Of course, my apologies, *Mr. Abernathy,* but Montague isn't in at the moment." I exchanged knowing glances with my friends, "We would be happy to hold on to it and have him look at it first thing when he returns."

"That would be lovely, thank you dear, but I do hope you mean your friend, here." He gestured to Isaac. "I wouldn't want a woman tampering with such a *delicate* process. Your kind is simply not cut out for work of this nature. Far too technical."

I bristled, the hairs on the back of my neck standing at attention. "Of course. I'll be sure to keep it in the capable hands of Isaac over here."

*You know, the same guy who nearly hit me over the head with a sandwich a few minutes ago. Naturally far more capable than a woman could ever be.*

Harvey turned the watch over to Isaac. Isaac's eyes flickered with mischief as he handed it directly to me. I smirked, Harvey glowered. *Checkmate.*

"And if you could just write down your address?" Isaac said, pushing away his smug look.

Harvey's distaste radiated off of him in waves. Gen handed him a slip of floral stationary.

Harvey pressed the pen a little too hard into the paper as he wrote, causing the ink to bleed rivulets and capillaries that jutted off of the words.

"With all due respect, young lady," he spat as he relinquished the paper into Gen's calmly expectant hand, "I'm not sure what a girl like you is doing in this line of work either. Shouldn't your kind be in *Los Angeles*? Or *Florida?* That's where all the *me-he-can-nos* flock, anyways." He all but spat the mispronounced word.

Gen froze. "*What?*"

"Oh, surely you know what I mean." He turned to Isaac. "Her presence here is inappropriate, is it not?" He shoved the paper into Isaac's hand.

"It's *not,*" Isaac all but snarled.

"I would have to say it is. Completely inappropriate. *Her* kind?"

"Her kind?" Isaac said, voice now deepening into a yell. "How dare you? How *dare* you?"

As soon as I saw Gen's muscles tense, she lunged toward Harvey. I grabbed her arm, pulling her back to my side.

"Kels, *please,*" she whispered, her eyes hot with rage.

"He's not worth it, Gen."

Isaac glared at Harvey. "He's not worth anything," he spat.

Gen swallowed hard, her angry facade quivering until it shattered. Red pushed its way into her cheeks, and I could see Isaac's rage intensifying.

"*Get out.*" Isaac's fury had turned suddenly quiet. He stepped between Harvey and Gen.

"Excuse me?"

"I said, *get out.*"

Harvey's face grew an alarming shade of red at this, and we watched through the crack in the door as he stormed down the street and back out into the afternoon light, waving the cane frantically as he fought to avoid stumbling.

As quickly as Harvey left, Gen turned, rushing down the hallway.

Isaac and I met eyes, then took off after her.

# CHAPTER NINE

I caught her arm just as she was about to run into our bedroom. "Gen, I–" my voice trailed off. *I'm sorry? It's not true?* I believed both of those things with all of my heart, but I didn't know what she wanted –or needed– to hear.

Isaac screeched to a halt beside me. "Gen," he said breathlessly.

She turned around, cheeks wet.

"I know this is scary, but we'll make it back home and it won't be like this anymore. Things can go back to normal, they can–"

"Isaac," Gen said, her voice tight. "Don't you get it? This *is* normal."

"What?" he said softly.

I wanted to contribute, but I couldn't find the words.

"It does happen. It's the exact same. Maybe I'm allowed to go to school, maybe I can have a job, but it's still the same."

Isaac squinted. "I don't understand."

"I don't expect you to," Gen said softly, her emphasis on the 'you' almost imperceptible. "But it's the things people say. Seeing the news, seeing everyone say that I should 'go back to Mexico.'" She looked up. "I was *born* in Gillonsville. And besides that, I'm not even Mexican, I'm Chilean, and I just…" She trailed off and took a deep breath. "I've never had a Latino teacher. I've never seen myself represented, besides negatively on TV. I constantly have to watch people caption Instagram posts in Spanish to be 'quirky.' I have to watch people wear my culture as a costume. And my music is never *music* it's *"Spanish"* music. And I can't do anything about it." She took another breath. "I want to strike back, but that only fuels their mindset. But if I walk away, so do they. I'm stuck." She closed her eyes for a long second, and when she opened them they were full of emotion I couldn't find the words to describe. "So, yeah," she finished, "maybe nobody tells me I only belong in Los Angeles or Florida in 2018. But they make it pretty clear that I don't belong in Gillonsville either."

"Gen, I'm sorry, I never–"

"Isaac." She cut him off, although her tone wasn't angry. "I can't do this right now. I'm sorry, but I can't."

She slipped through the door to our room, and closed it behind her immediately. A few seconds later, I heard the pins of the lock slide into place.

Isaac and I stood there for a moment, staring at the closed door. Isaac reached up to knock, but I pulled his arm back. "Not now." I began walking back toward the kitchen. "She needs time. You know Gen. When she has a problem, she needs to think through it. *Alone.*"

I could see the confliction dancing across Isaac's face. His instincts were programmed to comfort, that much I knew. It wasn't so much outright. It was the little things. Like when I fell down the stairs in fourth grade and broke my wrist. Gen was the pragmatist, running for my mother, reciting the steps of R.I.C.E. by heart when I came home. "*Rest, ice, compression, elevation,*" she would say over and over again. But it was always Isaac who brought over stacks of our favorite movies, replacing my ice packs with the same steadiness with which he replaced our popcorn. It was Isaac who gave me the Iron Man pillow he had owned since first grade on a strict loan, propping it under my arm before we settled in.

So, yes, it wasn't hard to understand why he seemed so drawn toward that door.

Finally, he stepped away, walking alongside me to the kitchen.

I wished I could transfer strength to him, like osmosis, or diffusion, whatever that science teacher I saw days that felt like years ago called it.

I felt the two poles of my life pulling me, pulling my heart thin. I could feel my heart strings straining. They felt taut and limp at the same time. A part of me felt pulled in Gen's direction. The other part of me was anchored to Isaac, a pull too strong for me to break.

The rock and the hard place were closing in on me, expanding as I did everything in my power to contract and escape.

As we rounded the corner into the kitchen, I met Isaac's eye. "I know that right now you're thinking about everything you can't do."

Isaac laughed dryly. "It's that obvious, huh?"

I sat down. "I think it's fair to say I know you pretty well. And with that, I think it's fair to say I know what could make you feel better. Gen's clearly feeling pretty overwhelmed right now. And while we can't take away the source of that, we can take away some of the excess stress. So, we should pick up where we left off. Give her some time to think through things while we get some work done." I dangled Harvey's watch above the table, before letting it fall with a metallic clang. "Should we crack this baby open?"

"Kels, there's no point."

"What would you suggest, then–"

"No, I mean there's no point to taking apart Harvey's watch. You heard him. He's just a customer. Why would Peter have given him a watch with powers?"

My eyebrows furrowed briefly, before a smile spread slowly across my face. "The door was locked."

"What?"

"When we got back from Margaret's. Gen locked the door to the shop."

"Why would that – OH! Oh." Now Isaac's smile matched mine.

"He broke in."

"He broke in," Isaac echoed.

A few minutes later, I had procured a wallet of tools from Peter's desk, double checked the locks on the shop's door, and returned to the kitchen.

Harvey's watch looked up at me from the table, and I eyed it as I sat down, feeling like a boxer sizing up his opponent.

I grabbed hold of the long, silver chain and pulled it, centering the watch in front of me. There, I noticed that it had a small, purple fleur-de-lis replacing the number twelve on the dial, just the same as ours. I turned the watch toward Isaac and pointed. "Look at that." I held out my own wrist. "Same as ours."

"Come on, Kels. It's probably just a maker's mark."

"Maker's mark?"

"You know. It's the 'signature move' of a manufacturer. Michael Jackson had the moonwalk, and Peter has the… well, the fleur-de-lis."

I scoffed. "Michael Jackson? How old are you? But, yeah, I guess you're right."

Flipping open the booklet of tools, I scanned for anything resembling a screwdriver. I pulled the desired tool out, and pressed it against the first screw holding the watch's face in place.

I turned it, then gasped as it slipped. I repositioned and tried again. This time, the screw began to move. Once I had removed all four, I took a deep breath, then lifted the face, and placed it aside.

A tightly wound scroll of paper sprung free from the watch, revealing a crescent shaped gap beside the gears. The scroll landed on the table about an inch from the watch.

I reached toward it hesitantly. I spread it flat against the table, and gasped.

The note itself made no sense, but yet I was terrified. The handwriting was looping, crawling, crooked.

The handwriting was Peter's.

# CHAPTER TEN

*Should you seek the purple moon:*
*Chambrelain,*
*Where the clock strikes two.*
*Know what you want,*
*And it will come to you.*

I read the lines several times, tracing over Peter's handwriting repeatedly with my finger. The words made no sense, but, beyond that, it made no sense for Harvey to have them. Why were they in his watch? Especially if he was trying to break in… Unease slipped its way into my mind, making my skin crawl.

"What on earth is that supposed to mean?" Isaac said abruptly, leaning equally as close to the paper as I was. "*Chambrelain?* That's not even a word!"

I squinted at the paper. "Do you think it means Chamberlain? Like, the name?"

"Maybe..." Isaac said. "It makes more sense than anything I can think of."

"Even if it says Chamberlain, I'd hardly say it makes sense. I mean, seriously: *Where* the clock strikes two? How can time be a *where*?"

Isaac took off his glasses and began to bite his lip. "Maybe we shouldn't try to figure it out."

"Why wouldn't we? Isaac, it's the only lead we have."

"No. We have this, and we have Harvey. Maybe it's not worth focusing on this poem, or whatever it is. Maybe we just need to find him instead."

"How do you expect to– Oh." I stopped mid-sentence as Isaac reached into his pants pocket, withdrawing a decidedly familiar piece of stationary.

"He wrote his address down, remember. I haven't looked yet, but I figured that if we checked the map we could... We could... You've got to be kidding me." Isaac's face was pale, with bright spots of red rising high on his cheeks. He stood up sharply, his chair grating against the stone floor. "Oh my god. Oh my god. We are not okay we are *so* not okay–"

I grabbed his arm, pulling him back into his chair. "Isaac, slow down. What's wrong?"

He shoved the floral stationary toward me, crossing his arms against his chest. "Look." He huffed out a long breath.

*Good luck, apprentices.*

The room was suddenly cold. My heart beat against the wall of my chest, and it felt as though my lungs would no longer take on air. The handwriting was sharp and angular, the letter I not so much dotted as it was slashed.

"I… I don't understand." My voice sounded rough, forced even.

"Kelsey," Isaac said, meeting my eyes. "We can't go looking for him. We just can't. He knows who we are and he knows what–"

"What's the difference?" I said, rising suddenly. "We're looking for Erindale, and so far as I can tell he's not exactly in our good graces. Be rational, Isaac."

Isaac looked down at the floor. "You sound like Gen."

"So are you saying she's right?"

Our heads snapped up in unison towards the doorway, and I saw Gen leaning against the frame, a smug smile plastered across her face. My eyes lit up.

"Gen!" I softened my tone. "Listen, I–"

"Yeah, yeah, save it," Gen said, crossing the room to lean forward, her elbows pressing against the wood of the table. "I'm not going to get anywhere if I listen to people like him."

I stared into her eyes intently.

She stared back. "Kelsey, I promise, I'm fine." She didn't sound fine, but her tone left no room for argument. "So, what'd I miss?"

Isaac's laugh was harsh. "We've got another lunatic on our hands. Remember how we had Harvey write down his address?"

Gen frowned. "What?"

I slid the paper to her. "Just look."

Isaac and I had panicked when we read the note, but I knew better than to expect such a reaction from Gen. I could see her mind switching to analysis, grasping for a hold. She whispered the words to herself. "*Good luck, apprentices.*" Then, louder: "How could he possibly know that? We have to find him."

"How?" Isaac said defeatedly. "This was supposed to be his address."

"We still have to find him," Gen snapped. "If he knows who we are to Peter, he has to have more information than most people. Don't be stupid, Isaac," she added. "We'll find him how we found Erindale. The customer log. He came in to have his watch repaired, so naturally he was a customer at some point." She paused when she saw the drawn looks painting our faces. "What?"

"Well, about the watch…" I gestured toward the dismantled object, and the piece of paper beside it. "I don't think he was really a customer." I explained our theory regarding the locked door. "And, beyond that, we found this poem in his watch. It's about the purple moon. We figured he wouldn't have it unless…"

Gen began to tap her foot frantically, looking around the room as if there could be answers within the walls. "Can I see it?"

We handed her the paper, and she skimmed it quickly.

"We're thinking that Chamberlain is a name," Isaac interjected. "We were about to check the journal and customer log."

"Okay," Gen said, nodding. "While we're in the customer log, I think it's worth a shot to look for Harvey's name. We don't want to miss anything important. He said he bought the watch about a month ago, so we can check there."

"Gen, I *really* don't think–"

"Is that worth missing our shot?"

A few minutes later, it became painfully clear that our suspicions had been correct. There was no record of any purchase under the name of Abernathy, nor of any watch which matched the description. I was beginning to feel trapped. The stone walls of the kitchen seemed to close in around me, pushing me into the cold wood of the table.

"So, no Harvey. What about Chamberlain?" Isaac turned to me, and I cracked the journal open to the back few pages.

"C... C... C..." I muttered. "Caron, Chambers... Chamberlain! He lives in Gillonsville."

"And, year?" Isaac said anxiously.

I smiled. "1811."

Gen leafed through the pages of the customer log. "So if Peter met him in 1811, he'd be in the customer log sometime around then."

The room was silent for a long moment. I leaned back in my chair, staring up at the ceiling. Long rows of wooden planks slanted their way across the surface, splinters hanging down like miniscule stalactites. I hadn't realized how panicked I had been until the simple action of counting the planks began to soothe me. *One, two, three, four, five.* The simplicity was a welcome reprieve.

Gen drew in a sharp breath, and I looked back down.

"Did you find something?" Isaac pressed.

"Sort of. It's in 1810, not 1811" Gen said uneasily, "but it's a Chamberlain. 122 Meadows Place."

"Meadows Place…" I tried to remember the layout of 2018 Gillonsville. Was it Meadows that connected to Main Street just past the coffee shop? I couldn't seem to place it in my mind, although it seemed fairly familiar. Just as I was about to give up, Isaac produced the map and spread it across the table.

It was wrinkled and stained from the rain, but it was still legible, albeit smudged. Ink splintered across the fibers of the paper where it had ran from the water, creating the illusion of extra miniature roads tracing their way into the city.

Gen's finger smacked down an inch or so from where I was looking. "Meadows Place, right there." She took her other hand, and slid it over my arm. "And we are… here. That doesn't look too far, does it?"

I looked out of the small window, then at my watch. "Not too far, no, but probably too far for tonight."

The sky was brushed with long streaks of pinks and purples, and the light had taken on a duskier quality.

"You're forgetting something else, Kels," Isaac added.

"What?"

"The rest of the poem. *Where the clock strikes two.* We can't go tonight. We have to go at two, like the poem says."

Gen rolled her eyes. "Isaac, are you stupid? That's not what that line means. You get it, right, Kelsey?"

I drew my eyebrows together, running a hand through my now loose hair.

"Seriously? Neither of you get it?"

"Enlighten us," Isaac said dryly.

"*122* Meadows Place. As in twelve-two." She groaned at our still blank expressions. "Twelve and two! The two numbers shown on a clock when it's two. Honestly." She huffed, and leaned back.

I laughed. "That's obvious to you?"

"And it's not to you?"

The laughter we descended into was cleansing. The tension from the past day which thickened the air seemed to dissipate, leaving us feeling wonderfully light.

"You have got to be the most pretentious person I've ever met," Isaac said, wiping his eyes. "*Twelve-two!*" He said mockingly, placing his hands on his hips in a remarkably accurate caricature of Gen. "It's *obvious.*"

"It's not my fault you two never pay attention!" Gen said, although she was laughing too, now. She took a deep breath, and a more serious expression returned. "So, Chamberlain. Should we go in the morning?"

I smirked. "I think we're better off waiting until two–"

"KELSEY JACOBSON FINISH THAT SENTENCE AND I–" Isaac couldn't even finish his sentence before he once again dissolved into laughter.

"I'm serious!" Gen protested. "Tomorrow morning?"

"Yes, Gen," Isaac said dutifully. "Tomorrow morning. But now is not tomorrow morning. Now, we're giving ourselves a break. It's too late to do anything else, and we don't need to research because we already have a plan. We're lightening up. Care to join us?"

"How are we supposed to lighten up?" Gen said, pulling at her sleeves nervously. "There must be something else for us to do. We could read the books more, or search the house. There's bound to be more research we could be doing, more clues, more–"

"–More ways for you to be annoying?" Isaac said with a grin. "Come on, it's fine, Gen. We *have* a plan. Yes, it's not written down in that absurdly color-coded planner of yours–"

"–It's not–"

"–Gen, we're thirteen. It's *completely* absurd. My point is, the plan is set." He clapped his hand around Gen's shoulder, and a smile could help but tickle her lips. "Tonight, we have fun."

She brushed his hand away. "And how do you suggest we do that?"

Isaac and I met eyes and he smiled. "Kelsey, do you know what I'm thinking?"

"No *way*," Gen said emphatically.

"A sing-along, Isaac?" I asked through a laugh.

Gen and I were standing beside a comically large grand piano, with Isaac seated at the bench.

He lifted the cover away, and brushed some dust from the keys. "I saw it earlier," he said casually. He stretched his fingers over the rows of black and white, hovering just above the porcelain.

Gen huffed an incredulous breath."Need some gloves, maestro?"

"I need only your cooperation, Genevieve. Requests, *s'il vous plait.*"

She rolled her eyes. "Your pronunciation is abysmal, Isaac."

"Fine," he declared. "Kelsey, then. Any ideas?"

I scoured my brain, but any ability to think was clouded over by my sheer confusion over the situation. Songs? Our lives were upside down. Isaac was sitting at a grand piano in 1811, our mentor was gone, likely at the hands of a rogue apprentice, and now... Songs? I smiled, in spite of myself. "*A Whole New World.*"

Isaac laughed. "True that." He pressed his fingers against the keys. "*A Whole New World* it is."

The throw rug on the floor became our magic carpet late into the night. My heart felt lighter, as if I really were flying. Maybe it was a whole new world. Maybe our lives were changed. But, for the first time in a long time, in that moment, I felt fairly sure everything was going to be okay.

# CHAPTER ELEVEN

When I woke up I was met with the altogether too-startling realization that I wasn't tired. That in and of itself was a miracle. The next miracle was the smell of eggs and toast which spilled into the room through an open door. I hastily combed through my hair with my fingers, pulling at the tangles fervently before giving up and working my hair into a loose braid. Throwing on a robe over the white cotton nightgown Gen had discovered in the back of the wardrobe, I followed my nose downstairs.

When I entered the kitchen I found Gen leaning against the counter, still steaming mug of tea in hand. Isaac sat catty-corner from her on the edge of the table, eating eggs straight out of the frying pan.

"G'Morning Kels," Isaac mumbled through a mouthful of eggs.

I crossed to the counter and retrieved my own fork,

then perched on the table across from Isaac. "So how'd you make all this?"

"Well," Gen interjected, before Isaac could speak. "I, being the domestic goddess I am-" She laughed at my arched eyebrow. "Yeah, obviously kidding. Isaac did it."

"Yes," Isaac said, brandishing his fork with a flourish, "I, in fact, am the domestic goddess of this establishment."

He had clearly gotten dressed in a hurry this morning, at least according to his partially unbuttoned shirt and messy hair. His eyes were dewy with sleep.

I swallowed my bite of scrambled egg. "They're good." I gave an appreciative smile.

"That's what I thought!" Isaac confirmed, hopping off the table. "Food of the soul my friend, food of the soul."

"Food of the soul?" Gen snorted, "What are you, scrambled egg Buddha?"

"Eggpiscopalian," Isaac fired back.

My fork squeaked as it scraped against the bottom of the pan.

"Eggs are gone," I reported.

Isaac began buttoning his shirt the rest of the way up, fingers fumbling all the way up. "Chamberlain time?"

Gen set her own plate in the sink, and leaned against the counter. "Well, I was thinking, and I'm not sure."

"What?" Isaac said, looking up from his buttoning. "Gen, you were totally for this last night."

"Yeah, I know," she admitted, looking almost sheepish, "but now I'm realizing the mission we're setting ourselves up for. I mean, we don't even know what the purple moon is. It seems like it could really be dangerous to rush into looking for something when we don't even know what that something is."

Isaac twisted his watch around his wrist, fidgeting with the metal strap. "I don't know what you want me to say, Gen."

I jumped in. "Look, I agree with Gen. Or at least I would, usually. It's crazy dangerous to go looking for something when we don't know what it is. Especially considering the only thing we know about it is that a probable kidnapper also wants it." I ran my finger across the fleur-de-lis of my watch, feeling the shape pressing into my fingertips. "But here's the thing. I've been looking in this journal non-stop since Peter left. There is nothing, and I mean *nothing* that's clarifying even the slightest idea of what it could be. So, in my eyes, the only way we can figure it out..." I took a deep breath, studying my friend's hesitant expressions. "Is to find it."

Gen began to pace, her shoes clicking against the stone as she traced a straight path from wall to wall. "But what if–"

"Gen!" I said suddenly, surprising myself. "We don't have *time* for what ifs. Yes, it's scary, and I know you don't like it when you don't have all the facts, but sometimes you just have to accept that you don't. I know you're strong enough to do that."

She nodded. "Okay, okay. You're right. It'll be fine." I was unsure of whether she was convincing me, or convincing herself.

"So, Chamberlain? Isaac, do you have the map?"

He gave a thumbs up.

The corners of Gen's lips twitched into a smirk. "Right side up this time?" I could still hear fear underneath her levity.

"Hey!" he yelled, although I saw him frantically double check. "Yes. It's all under control."

I looked at Gen once more, then turned to him. "Hey, Isaac." I scrambled, trying to come up with something believable. "I think I actually left the journal in Gen's and my room. Can you go grab it before we leave?"

He looked at me sideways, then suddenly, his face lit up with understanding. "Oh! Yes. Of course." He ran into the door frame on his way out of the room. "Coming right up!" he shouted over his shoulder.

Gen shuffled her feet against the floor, but smiled when she met my eyes. "What was that about?"

I looked at her seriously. "Gen. I'm not stupid. It's not like you to not want to go after something. There's something bothering you, and it's not this."

Gen's voice pitched higher. "I don't know what you're talking about."

"Gen, come on. I know you do. You can tell me. It's okay."

She mumbled something unintelligible, refusing to look up from her shoes.

"What?"

"I said what if he's like Harvey. Or Walter." When she finally met my eyes, hers were misty. "Kels... I can't do that again."

I bit the inside of my cheek. Hard. I figured this was the source of Gen's unease, but I had not gone so far as to figure out what I could say to her. I fought hard to maintain eye contact with her.

"Gen. I know it's hard. Or, actually, I don't know. I'm not going to pretend I do. But what I do know, and what I can see is how hard it is for you. But you have to understand that his hate comes from fear. Really, really ugly fear. But, in a weird way, that should make you proud. Proud that your identity, your culture, your origins are so complex, unique, and *powerful* that people like Harvey resort to *fearing* them. So, yes, it's terrible. And you have *every* right to be mad. But let that anger become fuel to your mission of educating people. And telling them that they're wrong." I added, laughing in spite of myself. "You've always been pretty good at that." The hints of a smile tickled Gen's lips. "You just can't be ashamed," I continued. "That's what he wants, what people *like him* want. The best way to prove those people wrong is to show them just how proud you are to be Latina."

Gen smiled. "I'll make sure he knows that."

"Good call. I know you can. And will," I added, smiling.

"Though she be but little, she is fierce," Isaac said, striding through the door. He picked the journal up off of the kitchen table, where it had been all along, and handed it to me. "Nice one, Kels."

"Who are you calling little?" Gen said, laughing. "But, thanks, guys. So, are we doing this?"

Outside, we struggled to follow the route which Isaac had traced on the map. Although technically accurate, the line was shaky, crooked and scratched in places where he had failed to master the art of the fountain pen.

However, despite it all, half an hour later we were standing next to what was, according to the simple black and white sign, 122 Meadows Place.

The house was simple. It looked as though it could be an architect's rendering of a toddler's drawing of a house. A square of yellow slatted walls reached up to meet a perfectly triangular top. The door was surrounded by white crown molding. The two windows on the face of the house had black shutters, all open. The property smelled slightly of grass and something mildly sour. It hardly seemed like the kind of place where a magical object would be stored.

"It's a bit… underwhelming." I couldn't help but voice my thought.

Gen nodded, but Isaac shook his head.

"Guys, can we not do this now?" Gen hissed and pointed to the house. "More important things to worry about right now."

She stepped forward and rapped sharply on the door.

I took an instinctual step toward her. "Gen, if you're worried about what he might say I can–"

"No, Kels. I've got this."

Isaac looked at me, slightly panicked, but I merely shrugged. I knew better than to tell Gen what she could and couldn't do.

Gen was about to knock again when the door began to swing open. The metal hinges shrieked as they were pulled revealing a man who looked to be about Peter's age peering around the door frame. His hair was sparse and gray, and wrinkles coated every inch of his face, painting the appearance of an almost permanent frown. Although he had peculiarly prominent cheekbones, skin hung low beneath them, giving him an almost jowled look. I wasn't close enough to know, but I could imagine that he smelled of tobacco. His already piercing green eyes grew impossibly sharper when he saw Gen. He looked over her shoulder to Isaac.

"If you wish to speak to me, it will be through the boy." His voice sounded like a rake being scraped over concrete, abrasive and rocky.

I saw Gen stiffen, and for a moment I thought she was ready to turn away and oblige. Then: "*No.*" The word was sharp. "No," she repeated, this time louder. "There is no reason you should want to speak to him anymore than me."

The man sighed, and began to close the door. Gen wedged her foot into the gap, and I winced in sympathy.

"What is it that makes you willing to talk to him but not me? If you can answer that while looking me in the eye without feeling ashamed, I'll gladly go." Gen held his steely gaze for what felt like almost a full minute.

I knew this version of Gen. Determined, strong-willed. Authentic.

The door opened, freeing Gen's trapped foot. She moved aside, gesturing for the man to join us on the small pathway to the house.

"Fine," he said, once he was standing beside us. "What is it that you want?" I noticed he still avoided looking directly at Gen, but in some morbid way it felt like progress.

We glanced at each other.

"Is your last name Chamberlain?" Isaac said abruptly.

The man nodded slowly. "But what does that mean to you?"

"Well that depends," Gen cut in. "Have you heard of a Peter Montague? Or anything about 'the purple moon?'"

A deep crease grew into Chamberlain's forehead. "Did he send you? I already told him, I don't know anything about Peter–"

"Stop" Gen help up a hand. "If you don't know anything about Peter, who do you think sent us?"

"Another man."

"Which other man?" I could hear fear edging into Gen's voice.

"You tell me!" the gravely-voiced man insisted. "He was here only a week or so ago, and he asked those exact same questions."

Isaac looked at me, fear deep-set in his hazel eyes.

Gen swallowed hard, and when she spoke again her voice was rough. "Did he say his name?"

"Yes, yes he did." Chamberlain stared at the sky. "What was it… Rodney… no, no, that's not right. Ronald? No, it wasn't– Oh yes. Rupert. It was Rupert. He didn't give a surname, though. Funny, that."

I couldn't catch my breath. *Rupert. Rupert was here. The second Erindale on our list had been to this very place. He was after the purple moon too, and when he couldn't find it...* I looked between Gen and Isaac frantically. They looked to be in similar states.

Isaac had grown alarmingly pale. His freckles stood out against his skin with harsh contrast. I could hear Gen's breathing growing faster.

The elderly man peered at us curiously. "Do you know him? You look terribly frightened."

Something overtook me. I couldn't explain it, I couldn't even begin to.

I took off, the ground pounding beneath my feet. I was running, although I didn't know my destination. The air was thin around me, and my breath came in cloudy bursts. I heard Chamberlain's gravely voice, which sounded like thunder as it boomed behind me. I didn't care. I just ran.

Before I reached the end of the block, I felt a hand clamp onto my shoulder. I gripped it, and was about to pry it off before I recognized it.

*Isaac.*

I released the hand. It remained on my shoulder. I could sense Gen's presence now too, but it was Isaac who spoke.

"Dude, why are you so freaked?

I took a deep breath, tried to slow down. Isaac's casual tone reminded me that it is was okay, would be okay. "He's closer than we are," I said, as level as I could draw up. "He already came here. He tried this a *week* ago!" I could hear my voice starting to pitch up, and I bit my lip hard. Another deep breath. "That's a lot of time to make up. A lot of time he's already had to figure out what the poem means."

"I know," Isaac said gently.

# CHAPTER TWELVE

Isaac and Gen granted me the luxury of relative silence until we were back within the confines of the watchmaker's. I slipped out of my black flats once we had passed the storefront. The cold stone bit roughly into my bare feet, but I didn't care. In fact, I relished the feeling. It was grounding, in a strange way.

I made for Gen and I's bedroom before either of my friends could get a word in edgewise. I hadn't realized my breath was trapped in my chest until I closed the door. I pressed my back against the wall and slid down until my knees were hugging my chest.

I had forgotten to lock the door, but I knew Gen. She wouldn't come in, not yet. Knowing her, she was probably standing outside the door, anxiously checking her watch, waiting for the appropriate time to make her entrance and attempt to pull me off of the floor and out of my funk.

I was embarrassed, if I was being completely honest with myself. The way I had acted at Chamberlain's… I wasn't proud of it. My cheeks burned as I recalled the exact moment I had begun to run. And what was I running from? The *idea* of Erindale? I couldn't think of something much more pathetic. And running wouldn't solve anything, anyways. He was ahead of us, and I thought the best way to fix it was to throw a tantrum. *Seriously.*

I heard the twist of the knob before the door opened. Gen slid down beside me, and placed her hand on top of mine. She studied my face for a few seconds, clearly classifying symptoms in her filing cabinet of a brain.

*Sweaty palms,* she had no doubt thought as she first touched my hand. *Red eyes, although her cheeks are dry. So not crying… yet, anyways. Diagnosis: Not okay.*

"I know it's scary," she said, finally. "But you said yes to this."

"I thought we'd still have the option to go home, you know–"

"No," Gen countered. "I mean *this.*" She gestured collectively. "You could have said no the moment I showed you that box and that note. But you didn't. You said yes. Do you know what that means?"

I squinted at her. "Should I?"

She sighed. "Don't you remember what Mrs. Allen said in English class? Come on, it was only the week before we left?"

"Gen… that feels like a lifetime ago. No, of course I don't remember."

"Of all the things I admire you for, your memory never was one," Gen said, the hints of a grin tickling her lips. "She said that a hero becomes a hero when they say yes to the opportunity for adventure."

I sat up straighter, pushing away from the wall. "I'm not a hero, if that's what you're getting at."

"Well, if you had listened to her, you'd know that's what every hero says."

"Gen, I–"

"No. Kelsey, you need to start believing in yourself. We've made it this far, so I know we're capable of this. Peter said it himself. So if you can't trust yourself, trust him. Or me. Either way, you need to realize that you can do this. That's non-negotiable."

I laughed. "Thanks, Gen."

"Of course." She stood up off of the ground, and offered her hand to me. "Now come on. We've got a mystery to solve."

As Gen led me back to the kitchen, her words simmered in my mind. *A hero.* I knew I wasn't that. I couldn't be. But something about what she had said resonated with me.

*You need to realize you can do this.* The phrase expanded like ripples on a pond until it consumed my entire conscious. *You can do this.*

When we returned to the kitchen, it was to see Isaac sitting alone, looking wildly small at the far end of the massive table.

I sat down across from him, Gen beside me. *You can do this,* I reminded myself. "So, the game plan. This proves it. Rupert Erindale is our guy, and he was most definitely looking for the purple moon. And, considering he made the same mistake we did, I'm willing to assume he didn't find it."

"Or maybe he did," Isaac said.

"No," Gen cut in. "If he had found it, he wouldn't have had a need to take Peter."

"That's one thing I don't get," I said, pushing my hair behind my ears. "He kidnapped Peter via time travel, or at least that's what it looked like. So why does he need the purple moon? If he already has a functional watch, what's the point?"

"An army of one is never as strong," Isaac said, pushing up his glasses. "If he's really trying to garner power, he won't want to be working alone. Him taking Peter is only evidence that he has one watch. If he wants more, it's only logical that he would want the purple moon. After all, I think it's pretty clear that it's the main power source for the watches. You probably need it to make more."

"So he took Peter because he couldn't find it." I nodded slowly as I spoke. "And yet, somehow, we're supposed to be able to find it."

"Apparently," Isaac said.

Gen twisted a strand of hair around her pointer finger. *Curl, release, curl, release.* "Can I see the poem?"

I reached for the journal, which still lay on the kitchen table where Isaac had dropped it. I plucked the slip of paper out of the front cover, and handed it to Gen. She muttered the words to herself.

"*Chamberlain,*" she repeated. "I can't understand what else that could mean. And the formatting is so weird. It's not even a phrase. Just… *Chamberlain.* The first note from Peter was so poetic. This seems out of character."

"Gen, it's a riddle for the location of a magical object," Isaac said pointedly. "I'm sure his focus was hardly on the principles of grammar."

"If that were true he wouldn't have rhymed it," Gen replied. "There's clear effort. So why just *Chamberlain.* Not 'with Chamberlain' or 'by Chamberlain.' Nothing."

Isaac buried his hand in his curls. "Maybe we're looking at it wrong."

"Oh, I have no doubt of that," Gen said. "But unless you know what we can do to be looking at it correctly, that doesn't get us very far."

As they were talking, I had begun to leaf through the journal once more. I wasn't reading, merely flicking through the paper. The journal wasn't completely full. A half a centimeter of clean paper was sequestered at the back of the volume, ready for Peter's newest exploits. I was about to turn back to the beginning when I noticed a tear in one of the last few pages. I turned to the page and my brow furrowed in confusion.

The page was full, but with what looked to be French. Ink coated every centimeter of the page, crammed in between the crevasses left by other words. "Gen," I said, pushing the journal toward her. "Look at this. Does it mean anything to you?"

Already fluent in Spanish, Gen had opted for French classes in high school, quickly becoming flawless in another language as Isaac and I struggled to conjugate *estar* or distinguish *yo, me,* and *mi,* much to Gen's amusement.

She scanned the page, and began to tap her foot. "No, not really. They're just random words. See that one?" She pointed to a word with a thick slash through it. "*Bois.* Wood. And that one–" –she pointed again– "–*Chambre.* Which means– HOLD ON."

Gen pulled the journal beside the poem. She looked frantically between the two. "OF COURSE!" she exclaimed. "*Montague.* A French last name. Oh my god, I can't believe I didn't notice. Of course! This would have been the perfect way to hide it from Erindale."

"Gen, I'm not following," I said carefully, although I couldn't completely mask my excitement.

"It's not Chamberlain!" Gen said, almost shrieking now. "It's *chambre lain.* It's French! I thought the spacing looked weird, but I never questioned it. If it weren't for Peter's ridiculous handwriting–"

"Gen," Isaac said excitedly, "what does chambre mean?"

Gen broke into a wild grin. "Bedroom."

My heart began to race once more, although this time it was not from fear. The tension surrounding the three of us was palpable as we all but ran out of the kitchen, rushing into Peter's bedroom.

"It has to be in here," Gen said, looking around the room.

We immediately began to dig through the room. Isaac pulled at the desk drawers, peering within each one. I looked under the bed, then in the small closet in the corner. Gen pulled out books from the bookshelf.

A few minutes later, we had found nothing.

The shiny excitement of discovery had begun to dissipate, at least for me. Another failed attempt. I felt defeated. I was tired of the highs and lows, tired of the way in which success continued to taunt us. Then, suddenly–

"Wait a minute. Get out."

Isaac's words surprised me.

"What?" Gen asked.

"Get out," Isaac repeated. "Stand in the doorway."

Gen frowned. "If this is some kind of joke…"

Isaac pouted. "When was the last time I was anything but serious, Gen? Come on."

Gen put her hands on her hips, but moved to stand behind Isaac in the doorway. "Ok, so when do you pull the quarter out from behind my ear?"

Isaac ignored her. "Just look at the floorboards."

Unlike the rest of the house, Peter's floors were hardwood. The twelve planks spanned out from a central point underneath the bed, reaching out to the walls of the room like spokes on a bicycle, or…

"Oh my god," Gen said through a breath. "It's a clock. *Where* the clock strikes two."

My jaw dropped. "It's under the second floorboard."

Isaac and I immediately rushed toward the plank, dropping to the ground, but Gen remained fixed to her spot.

"Gen, what are you waiting for?" Isaac was practically vibrating with energy. "We found it! *You* found it!"

"I'm as excited as you are, but– hey, I am!" she exclaimed, noticing Isaac's skeptical gaze. "I am excited, I promise. But we can't just yank up a floorboard. We need to find some tools."

I had almost begun to stand, when I suddenly changed my mind, falling back onto my heels. I twisted my dress in between two fingers, thinking. "No, I don't think we do."

"Kelsey, when I said for you to be confident I didn't mean that you should completely ignore logic."

"No, no, this isn't ignoring logic at all. Gen, if Peter was hiding an important magical object under these boards, he wouldn't make it take an arm and a leg to pull it up."

I slid across the wood, moving to the end of the second beam, where screws secured the plank into the ground. I closed my fingers around the metal, and pulled experimentally. Instantly, the screw slid free.

I held it up. "See? They're not screws. They're just pins." I grinned. "Easy access."

Now Gen joined Isaac and I on the floor, pulling away the pins, which resided in sets of two about every three feet or so down the board.

Once all of the pins sat in a small pile on the ground, I turned to Gen. "Care to do the honors? You did solve the poem, after all."

Gen looked as though she was about to say yes, but then something in her face shifted. "No. Let's do it together."

We surrounded the board. Gen was on the left, I was on the right, and Isaac was holding up the far end.

"I really hope you're right about this," Isaac added, although he didn't sound as though he felt particularly uncertain.

"I will be," Gen said, tightening her grip around the lip of the board.

"Okay," I said. "Three, two... one!"

We all lifted in unison, thrusting the plank aside so it lay a few feet away from the now gaping hole in the floor.

We all crowded over the opening.

I couldn't help but shriek.

Gen clasped her hand to her chest, looking almost dizzy with relief.

"This is it," Isaac said softly. "This is it! This is it, this is it, this is it!" His voice crescendoed rapidly, and he jumped up and down, pumping his fist in the air.

When could finally tear my eyes away to look up, I could see a purple glow illuminating his socked feet. The opening in the floor was filled with slender crescent moon shaped pieces of purple stone, the same color as the fleur-de-lis on all of our watches. The stones were radiant, glowly, and I half expected to be able to warm my hands over them like a fire.

Gen gasped again. "Guys, look!" She held up a piece of Peter's signature stationary, all floral and delicate. "This was in there."

I leaned in close to read it.

*Use it well.*

Now I joined Isaac, jumping to my feet, dancing with the sheer relief. I started laughing and couldn't stop. Soon, Gen and Isaac laughed with me, until we were eventually reduced to a sweaty pile on the floor, tangled in each other's arms.

"Gen," Isaac said, pushing my hair away from his face. "You are a genius. You are a complete and total genius."

Gen beamed, glowing almost as much as the stones.

We stayed in that position for a few minutes longer, before finally separating, falling back onto the floor.

I glanced back over at the pile of purple stones. "Someone pinch me."

"Sorry, can't," Isaac said, feigning an apologetic tone. "I'm too busy pinching myself."

"Ditto," Gen said.

Isaac leaned closer to the pile. "They're so beautiful," he said, reverence shining in his eyes. "How do you think we use them?" As he spoke, he subconsciously reached out toward the stones, pressing his hands into the stack.

"Isaac, no!" Gen and I both exclaimed, reaching out to pull him away.

I saw Gen disappear before I felt it, before I felt myself being jerked up into the air as Isaac's shot upward, fist still closed around a handful of the stones.

The sensation of being squeezed into a soda bottle, while simultaneously being pulled apart like string cheese. I felt as though cold water was lapping at my sides, rapidly rising until I couldn't breathe, until I was drowning in invisible water.

I recognized it with daunting trepidation: The sensation of time travel.

My fear and relief clashed like swords in my mind, metallically conflicting and forcing me to cringe. As I began to grit my teeth against the sensation, I was met with only one thought.

*Here we go again.*

# CHAPTER THIRTEEN

The sensation subsided and the room came into focus. My sight came back before the rest of my senses, and I scanned the room. We were still in the watchmaker's and Isaac and Gen's voices came from what sounded like underwater.

First slowly, then all at once, I broke the surface and their voices returned with blunt clarity.

I immediately whirled around. "What just happened?" I was surprised by how out of breath I felt.

Gen looked furious. "Why don't you ask *Isaac?* Of course! Of course you couldn't wait to give us the time to think out a plan! You just had to touch it, didn't you? And now we're stuck god knows *when*–"

"Gen, shut up!" Isaac exclaimed.

When I looked at him his eyes were wild, and his hair looked even more unkempt than average.

"No!" she said vehemently, almost shouting now. "You

don't get to try to justify this! There is nothing in this whole universe that could make me–"

"Nothing," Isaac said, raising an eyebrow.

"Yes, nothing because–"

"Oh, dear Genevieve, we have reached quite the milestone. For the first time in your life, *you* are the one missing what is plainly obvious to *me*."

"What are you talking about?"

Isaac held up his wrist and tapped the face of his watch.

I looked down at my own.

"No way," I whispered.

Gen looked up at me and followed suit, and soon she chorused her own "No way."

"We are *not* that lucky," I marveled.

The year dial on the watches had changed. An eight turned to a nine. A one turned to a five. A one turned to a two. 141 years.

It was 1952.

Suddenly the facade of awe broke. Gen punched the air and whooped loudly, and I could only laugh in my relief.

She pulled us both into a crushing hug, and I could feel the tension leaking from our bodies as she sighed in relief.

"Thank *God*."

Isaac smirked. "Don't you mean thank *you*? As in thank *Isaac?*"

"Isaac," Gen began slowly. "While I do forgive you, I refuse to believe that you could have planned this."

Isaac opened his mouth to protest, then closed it. "Alright, so it was an accident."

"No, no," Gen corrected. "Things don't work like that. Everything happens for a reason." She chewed on her lip. "Kels, what was the second half of the poem?"

"Know what you want, it will come to you." I recited the lines by heart. It no longer felt as though I needed to work to recall them, rather as though it were a tap that I turned on, the words rushing free as soon as the pressure was released.

Gen steepled her hands under her chin, and closed her eyes. She muttered the words to herself. *Know what you want, it will come to you. Know what you want, it will come to you.* She looked up sharply. "Isaac, what were you thinking about when you touched the stones?"

Isaac squinted. "Why does that–"

"Just answer the question."

Isaac took his glasses off and rubbed them on the silk scarf which still hung around his neck. "I was thinking about rescuing Peter. What else?"

Gen furrowed her eyebrows, and mumbled something under her breath.

I leaned in. "What?"

She looked up. "That would be to easy."

"What would?" Isaac asked.

"You were thinking about rescuing Peter. Now we're here, and we can rescue Peter."

"I don't follow," Isaac said, sucking in his cheeks.

"You knew what you wanted. It came to you."

"So–"

"So maybe the purple moons are like touchstones.

Maybe all you have to do is think about where you want to go, and touch them."

"That doesn't make any sense," I cut in. "How would that work in the watches?"

Gen held up her wrist, and pointed.

I followed the line of her finger and when I saw where it lead I couldn't help but gasp."The fleur-de-lis."

"I'm almost sure of it," Gen said excitedly.

I looked at the stone, and smiled. Of course.

Suddenly, I frowned. "But, wait, that can't work. I rub mine when I'm nervous." I felt suddenly self-conscious. "But… I've never been sent here."

Gen tapped her foot. "I would think not. Peter wouldn't make it that easy to access the powers when they're in the watches. But he did something that sent us back as soon as we put them on in 2018…" She shook her head. "I don't know."

Isaac had been unusually quiet. He was tracing his index finger around the circumference of his watch, but now he met Gen's eyes. "So what now?"

"We find Erindale," Gen said confidently. "We're in the right year. Relatively speaking, we might as well be on his doorstep."

"Do we hole up here, then?" Isaac leaned back. He glanced at the floorboard where the moons had been stashed before. The pile was exposed, and the moons still glinted back at us.

I was about to respond when I heard a shout coming from outside the door. My heart began to pound, and when I spoke it came out as a small squeak. "Who is that?"

Gen immediately stood. "We have to go find out."

"No," I hissed. "What if it's Erindale? Gen, you know better than to rush in blind. We need a plan."

I heard the shout again, this time closer, and I tasted metal.

Isaac's voice came in a whisper that was barely anything more than a breath. "Uh… guys. Not good."

I grasped at invisible straws with desperation as my eyes raced across the room. Peter's bed, his desk. There was a closet, but I doubted it was large enough to house all three of us. Then… one window, high on the back wall. *Window.*

"Gen, grab that chair. Drag it over there." Her eyes looked puzzled, but she did as I requested. The wooden desk chair scraped against the floor as she positioned it.

Before I got up, I hoisted the floorboard back over the purple moons. I didn't have time to replace all of the screws, so I merely wished the few I slid into place would be enough.

Gen jumped up onto the chair, and worked at the latch of the window. It hissed when it popped open.

"Isaac, boost!" Gen's tone was hurried. He made a basket for her foot with his hand then hoisted her out of the small window. I heard a crunch and a groan as Gen landed on the other side.

I stepped into Isaac's hands next, squeezing through the small window, praying I wouldn't fall on top of Gen.

Thorns bit into my back, but I quickly rolled off.

*Who plants rose bushes right below a window? Honestly, it's like they didn't even consider that one day teenagers might need to escape.*

Seconds later, Isaac dropped down onto the now slightly crushed bushes, and the window flapped shut behind him.

"That was close," I reflected breathlessly. "Too close."

We heard the shouting again, but this time the voice was clear. "Do you know what that was, Montague?"

Gen's eyes met mine. "*Montague,*" she whispered. "Peter."

She turned back toward the window. "He's in there! We have to go save him, we have to–"

"Gen, no!" Isaac caught her arm. "It's not safe. We're not just risking ourselves if we do this. We're risking Peter too. Is that worth it to you?"

Gen looked at her shoes woefully. "No," she mumbled.

We paused as a police car flew past. Its siren rang loudly, reverberating in my core, and my heart chilled. In the moment it passed, I felt blissfully invisible.

"So," Isaac said clearly. "We need to make a plan. A plan to do this *safely.*"

"And protect the purple moons," I added. "If it's Erindale in there, we run the risk of him finding them."

"But, Kels," Gen reasoned, "the floorboard was moved aside. He probably already did."

I tugged on a few loose strands of my hair. "No. No," I repeated, "he didn't. It's like Peter said. Things instantaneously occur between the past and the present. That board didn't move until we moved it in 1811."

"Which means it got put back right away," Isaac finished, realization crossing over his expression.

Gen nodded, slowly at first, then faster. "Okay. Okay. You're right. So we don't have to worry about that. Probably.

Where do we go, though?" She darted her eyes back to the back of the watchmaker's. "We kind of lost our batcave."

I puzzled for a moment, before a wide grin spread its way across my face. "I know just the place."

We walked parallel to the back of the storefronts before finding a small alley between two shops. I took a deep breath, then entered. The alley was musty and dark, bearing a harsh contrast to the sight when we emerged through the other side.

I squinted against the harsh daylight, but when the world came into focus I felt as though I could cry.

The street came with a sight I felt as if I hadn't seen for a wildly long amount of time. A teal corvette slinked its way down the road, its polished metal gleaming in the sunlight. A car. I could barely believe my eyes. An actual car. A vehicle with horse*power* instead of just horses.

I would feel stranger for being so excited about the prospect if it weren't for the fact that when I finally turned back my friends' dropped jaws mimicked mine.

I trailed my eyes across the surroundings. The formerly cobblestone road was now paved a slick black, and the muted blacks, browns, and tans of 1811 Gillonsville were replaced with bright reds, purples, and electric blues. Neon lights snaked across letters and lit up the previously only oil-lamp-illuminated streets.

A girl stood on an apple crate waving a sheaf of flyers frantically. "Buy a goat from Cunningham's! Goats for sale!"

I set off down the sidewalk, Gen and Isaac following, and visions of our eighth grade production of *Grease* assaulted my memory. The groomed lawns, classic cars, and gossiping housewives painted the perfect picture of 50s American life, a picture I thought too stereotypical to possibly be true.

If there's one thing I've learned from being an amateur time traveler it's that things in history have a general tendency to be just about what you expect them to be.

The feeling was reminiscent of coming back to school in the fall. Everyone was more or less the same, but everyone had gone through a few slight changes, rendering them just different enough for it to be incredibly unfair to call them the same. Maybe Will got glasses, or maybe Ryan's hair grew a couple of inches. Whatever it was, it certainly wasn't the same.

It felt as though I were seeing a billboard, advertising someone's ability to visit a historical site.

I'd always seen these signs as being a bit unfair, because you can't visit where the Kennedy assassination happened. You can visit the same road, and stand in the same places the people stood, but you can't go where they went. Going somewhere isn't a physical experience, at least not alone. People make places just as much as the concrete, the buildings, the trees.

Even time travel can't break that rule. The second you're there, you've changed the event. It's no longer the event you'd heard about. It's the event you're living.

As we continued down the sidewalks past rows and rows of pastel cookie-cutter houses, I failed to see an end to my dissociation.

"It feels like I should be singing *You're The One That I Want* or something," Isaac noted as we walked past a very John Travolta-esque Ford Convertible.

"Man, that was fun," Gen said, nostalgia evident in her brown eyes. Nostalgia in 1952 felt a bit ironic.

"Ah, to be John Travolta. I rocked that leather jacket. At least Danny had some fashion sense," Isaac said, smiling.

"You mean the jacket Jake found at Goodwill? Dude, it cost 50 cents. Not exactly high fashion." I joked.

"I beg to differ," Isaac said, "I rocked each and every last one of those 50 cents. Plus, you're one to talk about fashion. I think you're forgetting your *excellent* wig, Sandy."

"Touché," I laughed, giving a dramatic shudder. "It was the *worst*."

"Jokes on you guys," Gen taunted, "I told you you should've been in the crew."

"And give up all the glamor of a middle school acting career?" Isaac retorted.

As our laughter faded out, I further drank in the sights around me.

Neon signs hung from almost every shop, their blockish letters all proclaiming different messages.

A bright blue one advertised a laundromat.

A fluorescent orange let me know I should "Get my shoes shined here!"

A fire engine red one told me Marissa's Horse Supply Store was "The best in town!"

My eyes continued to scan the rows of neon before I was met with the sign I desired.

It was yellow, mounted on red backing, proclaiming two glorious words: Kelly's Diner.

I was met with another wave of nostalgia which left me reeling. Last time we were in that spot… I couldn't bring myself to fully articulate it. We were so carefree, so innocent. I both scorned and longed for that version of myself, criticizing my naivete while craving the sweet respite of purity.

I could never be that me again. For that, I hated her.

My scorn left me the moment a french fry entered my mouth, grease coating my taste-buds, preparing them for the tinge of salt I knew so well. The fries were still good. Very *very* good. I made my feelings known to Isaac and Gen.

"Heaven you say? Gimme." Isaac set down his BLT and snatched a fry from my plate.

"Hey, you had your own!"

"Yeah," Isaac said, his voice muffled through the potato. "What about it? I'm crowdsourcing."

"And what were the results?" Gen said, sipping her Diet Coke.

Isaac swallowed the bite with a sip of iced tea and a smile. "Five stars. Heaven confirmed." He overdramatically adjusted his glasses, as if for emphasis.

Gen raised her straw to her lips. The plate once been entirely blanketed in a blueberry pancake now lay clean beside her elbows with the exception of a few stray amber smears of maple syrup.

She swallowed hard, then looked carefully at me. "So, the plan?"

I raised my milkshake to my lips, chewing on the straw even after I had sipped. "Well, it seems like Peter is still in the watchmaker's. But what about the other voice?" I could feel fear settling in my stomach among the fries, making it churn uneasily. "Do we think it's Rupert?"

Isaac nodded, but didn't meet my eyes. "Who else could it be? And the way he talked to Peter.. There was something in his tone that I really didn't like."

A loud voice broke through the silence. "What is *she* doing here?"

Our heads all turned to see a tall man in a blue, short-sleeved button down, scowling in our direction. The hostess, a young, blonde woman stood with her jaw hanging slightly open in a never-delivered reply.

"I said," the man repeated, thrusting one thick finger in Gen's direction. "What is *she* doing here?"

My pulse quickened, and I turned to Gen. Her jaw was clenched and her face flushed red.

"Just because their *kind* is petitioning for education doesn't give her a right to come into this diner. Diners are an *American* tradition, and I won't have this one contaminated by–"

His voice was cut off by one which seemed unusually familiar, but with a deeper bass note. "Is there a problem, Dennis?"

A hand clapped around the first man's shoulder, and I traced the arm back to the face. These booths. The room. The counters. The smells. It was only natural.

The man standing before was, at least sort of, our Mr. Kelly from 2018. He had the same hair, except for 'this version' had a few streaks of gray and no beard, almost identical eyes, and a nose just slightly wider. It was almost like a spot the difference puzzle. The man was practically Mr. Kelly, or, our Mr. Kelly anyways.

"Mr. Kelly," the man responded, "you can't seriously suggest that it's okay for someone like her to eat here." He met his eyes almost knowingly. "Someone who's... you know."

"I quite certainly do *not* know," Mr. Kelly said. "I know what you're *implying*, but I have to say I find you entirely incorrect. With that attitude, in fact, I would suggest it is not she who is contaminating this diner, but, rather, you."

Dennis grew impossibly red. "But, she... I... You can't possibly–"

"I actually *can* possibly, and not only that, but I *will*. Get out of my diner, Dennis. Come back when you can figure out how to offer people some semblance of human decency."

Dennis stormed out, the tinkle of the bell over the door dull as he slammed it behind him.

Mr. Kelly scanned the diner, looking out upon a sea of gaping eyes. "Well, go back to your meals, all of you. You're paying me for food, not a spectacle." He looked toward the hostess. "You too, Kathy."

He sighed, then walked toward out table. "How's the grub treating y'all this fine afternoon?"

"Thank you for doing that, Mr. Kelly," Gen said quickly.

"Why, I haven't even introduced myself! Then again, I guess it's in the name. A smart girl, aren't you?"

"Are you ok?" The man's voice trailed off, a crease which was also distinctly familiar forming in between his eyebrows. The same smile.

Isaac shot me a look that had 'I'm betting on grandfather' written all over it.

I shot back a look involving a raised eyebrow which I hoped read 'Or slightly older twin.'

"I really am sorry about that," Mr. Kelly said softly. "Consider this one on me."

Gen spoke before I could. "You really don't have to do that, I–"

"I do have to," the man said firmly. "People may not pay me for a spectacle, but they do pay me for a place to eat. And eating is a thing to be done in peace. *It's on me.*"

Gen smiled. "Okay. Okay. Thank you so much, sir. Would you mind if we held the table for a few more minutes?"

Mr. Kelly smiled. "Of course." He walked away.

"So, are you wanting the check then?"

I felt my heart sink as I turned toward Gen. "Gen, I'm sorry. I didn't think this would happen again."

Gen laughed dully. "Kels, it's the 1950s. You probably should have expected it."

I flinched slightly.

"Really," she said, looking me in the eyes. "I'm fine. I can handle this. Do you really think–"

Before she could finish, a voice of a different calibre caught our attention. "Mr. Erindale, Mr. Erindale! You stay right here!"

I looked up to see a boy in a black leather jacket sliding through the glass doors of the diner, pursued by the shouting man.

Without another word, we stood and followed.

# CHAPTER FOURTEEN

"Mr. Erindale! Mr. Erindale, hold on for a moment!" A white aproned employee was chasing after the black haired boy in a leather jacket.

I looked up. "Did he just say…"

The leather jacketed object of his chase took the stairs exiting the diner two at a time, as if he couldn't even hear the voice pursuing him.

"Leonard! Leonard Erindale! Do not leave this building!"

"Wait, what?" Isaac's speech was the only thing hesitating, the rest of him still continuing to follow the evident game of cat-and-mouse going on. "Leonard?"

The cat slowed, even though the mouse was still walking towards the doors.

"Who is that?"

The waiter turned around, visibly flustered. "He didn't pay his check! When I handed him the bag he just took it and left."

I gave a soft sigh, then channeled every ounce of ferocity I had in me, which, not to brag or anything, was probably equivalent to that of a yorkie. "But *who* is he?"

Surprisingly enough, a yorkie was sufficient for the waiter. "Leonard Erindale," he said, stumbling slightly over his words, "His name is Leonard Erindale. Leo, his friends call him. He goes to my school, when he bothers to show up. This isn't the first time he's stolen food. My boss said that he'd fire me if I let him get away with it again…"

"Do you have any idea where he's going?"

"Probably behind the gas station across the street," the boy stuttered. He was a regular deer in the headlights. "He and his friends go there a lot." The waiter looked more nervous suddenly. "I wouldn't follow him."

I believed the waiter. If I was getting the right impression of this Leo guy, then I hoped there weren't too many of his 'friends' around.

"Man, you sure were scary back there," Isaac whispered with a smirk as we walked away.

"Hey," the employee called after us. "If you do go over there, tell him to bring ten dollars back here!" He tripped over his words.

I almost laughed. "Will do." I turned back to Isaac. "Don't criticize! I didn't see you trying to get the 411."

I could hear Gen behind us, still reassuring the waiter.

"You could've thanked him," Gen whispered, matching her stride to ours as she walked up beside me.

"Overrated," I said, trying to sound a little bit less guilty than I felt.

"I swear," Gen said, sighing, "Your manners are appalling. Anyways, let's figure out what this 'Leo' is about."

I looked across the street to the gas station and, courtesy of the smiling mechanic on its logo, it looked back.

"That's not creepy," I noted.

"Nope," Isaac said, cringing slightly.

Despite the cartoon mechanic's stare, when the steady traffic broke, we crossed the street. The lone taxi remaining honked at us, and the driver yelled something indistinct by means of words, but distinct by means of intention.

An attendant in greasy overalls opened the door to the small store behind the gas pumps as we approached, but I smiled and shook my head, hanging a left.

I was suddenly struck with a pang of fear. I definitely wasn't the type to hang out behind gas stations.

We weren't even all the way behind the white cement block structure, and already the ground was practically coated in cigarette butts.

The squashed white and yellow paper formed a clear trail leading behind the store.

Isaac kicked at a small pile of the discarded sticks. "It's like the freaking yellow brick road back here. What are they trying to do, get to the Emerald City?"

I laughed for a split second, then threw a hand over my mouth.

"Who's there?"

Apparently a split second was too long.

"Is that you, Caroline?"

Unfortunately not. Something told me Caroline might have earned a warmer welcome.

I mustered every ounce of fight in me, then I turned the corner, wishing I was Oz the Great and Powerful instead of just the Cowardly Lion.

"You're not Caroline." Leo's tone had no heat behind it.

"No, but you're Leo."

I turned to Isaac, eyes wide, but he dismissed me with a minute shrug.

"I have to wonder how you knew."

Gen stepped in this time. "That waiter wasn't exactly being subtle back there. Hate to be the bearer of bad news, but I'm *fairly* sure you owe him ten dollars.

"That's also true. Unfortunately, for Lucas, I have absolutely no intention of paying." Leo leaned back against the block wall. "Either way, you seem to know me pretty well, so it's time for your side of the introductions."

"Kelsey, Gen, and Isaac," I said, motioning to them in turn.

"Well, it's nice to meet you, Kelsey-Gen-and-Isaac." He said our names like they were one word. "What can I do for you?"

His pattern of speech would have been formal if it weren't for the casual lean he was maintaining against the back of the building.

"Well that depends. Are you related to a Rupert Erindale?"

Leo groaned, and I knitted my eyebrows.

"Oh, it's nothing," he said, rolling his eyes. "My father. What mess did he get himself into this time?" I could see something suspicious creeping into his nonchalance, and it unsettled me.

I glanced at Gen.

"What do you mean, this time?" Gen pressed.

"Well if you're looking for him, you probably know, so why don't you tell me, Kelsey-Gen-and-Isaac?"

I hesitated, but in my head my answer was complete. Magic watches? Kidnapping? His father wasn't exactly all that much of a model citizen.

"Because of Peter Montague." I took a chance.

All the color drained from Leo's face, and he stiffened slightly against the white wall.

"How do you know about that?"

I poked my shoe at a crack in the asphalt. "It depends. How much do you know?"

He looked around before answering. "Answer my question first."

I stopped poking at the crack.

Gen stepped forward, and placed her hands on her hips. "We're his–"

I pushed her back. "We're… indebted to him," I concluded. "Yeah. Indebted."

"You don't sound so sure."

I could feel heat rush into my annoyingly pale cheeks.

"You're right," Leo agreed, despite me having said nothing for him to agree to. "I suppose we've all got a few scores to settle. But, unfortunately, I can't tell you what I know until you tell me more about your relationship with this 'Peter' who I may or may not have information about. What's Peter to you?" He squinted at us. "Uncle? Grandpa? Pissed you off? Saved your life? All of the above?"

Isaac laughed. "Thank god it's not all of the above."

Leo shook his head, chuckling. "True. Though, judging by your answer, I take it none of those are right. Why do you care?"

Gen snorted, her black curls falling in front of one eye. "So the only way we're allowed to care about someone is if they're one of those things."

Leo scratched his chin, as if searching for stubble. Judging by the tiny, but fresh, cut by his left ear, I doubted he would find anything.

"We're his apprentices," I blurted.

Leo's eyebrows shot up. "Apprentices. That's interesting." I could see him fighting to regain a neutral expression. "Well, in that case, I have a wager."

Gen stepped forward. "Yes?"

"You will come back to my house with me and play a game of pool."

"What?" Gen's lips pressed into a frown.

"Pool? With cues? You know…" He mimed the movement of taking a shot.

Gen rolled her eyes. "Thank you very much. I know what pool is. But why are we playing it?"

"If you win, I'll tell you whatever you want to know about my father. If you lose, we go our separate ways."

"What?" Gen's mouth gaped open. "We can't go to your house! What about your dad?

Leo rolled his eyes. "My dad?" He kept his tone substantially incredulous. "My dad has things to do besides sitting around the house all day. He's a criminal after all, and if you know anything you know criminals don't like to be sitting ducks." He paused before clarifying. "He won't be home until late."

"Your mom?" Gen tried.

Leo raked a hand through his hair, feigning exasperation. "Would you guys calm down? I've got it under control. We've got the house to ourselves, I promise, but if you must know, my mom is gone."

"Gone, like divorce?" I asked.

"No, gone like dead," Leo said plainly.

My face dropped.

"Don't look so shocked, I was five when it happened. Car crash." Emotion flickered over his face for just a second, before it returned to its placid default. "She lost control and drove straight into the ocean. Never found the body. That's what the cops said." He leaned back in his chair, then sighed. "Stop looking at me like that. I don't even remember her."

The silence hung thick in the air until I straightened up, regaining my composure. "Empty house?"

"Besides the ghosts," Leo said, his voice a blank monotone.

I blanched, blood rushing out of my face. "The what?"

Leo's facade suddenly shattered into a million tiny pieces which fell away until a smug smile replaced the blank look. "My god, you're gullible."

"Wait, so there-"

"Obviously not!" Leo exclaimed. "Yes, the house will be empty. No ghosts, no parents, no one but us four. Are you in?" Leo moved to stand, shrugging as he did. "You can say no." He pulled his jacket tighter around his shoulders.

"No!" Gen said quickly. "No." She glanced at me and Isaac frantically. "You're on."

"Fair enough."

Leo descended the bleachers and began to walk.

After Leo was a couple of feet away. I turned to Isaac and Gen. "What?" I whispered. "His *house*? Are you crazy?"

"Are you coming or not?" Leo had paused, and he was looking over his shoulder, eyebrows raised.

"We'll catch up," Gen shouted back

Evidently satisfied, Leo continued walking.

As I began to walk, Isaac hissed in my ear. "Do you really think this is a good idea?"

"No," I whispered back. "But Gen seems pretty sure."

She was a few steps ahead of us, already pumping her shorter legs to keep up with Leo.

Isaac laughed. "Isn't she always."

Knowing I had left no room for denial, I sped up my pace, following the invisible trail of question marks Leo had left behind.

# CHAPTER FIFTEEN

After a walk which put us in the middle of a rather wealthy subdivision called Lester Heights, Leo stopped. "This is it. My humble abode."

I let out a long low whistle, eyeing up a three story mansion thoroughly adorned with large, sweeping windows. "Humble wouldn't be my word of choice."

"I can't help but notice you sound surprised," Leo said, starting up the concrete walkway leading to the front door. "Is it the jacket? Please tell me it's not the jacket."

"What?" I said, startled. "No, it's, uh, not the jacket, it's just…"

"Just what?" Leo asked. I could hear his expression even though his back was to me. "Is it the gas station?"

"Yeah, sure," I agreed, though that wasn't exactly what I was getting at.

"Whatever," Leo scoffed, "I'm just glad it's not the jacket. Not to be overzealous, but I look great in this thing."

I scoffed a bit myself. "Do you consider yourself to be as humble as you consider your house?"

Leo dug into the pockets of the aforementioned jacket, fishing out a set of house keys. "Humility is for the indecisive. I'm just efficient." Leo punctuated the statement by unlocking the door. He swung the door open, leaving a leading arm in the entryway. "Ladies first."

My mind twitched toward confrontation until he smiled broadly, and his eyes twinkled with humor.

All sarcasm was forgotten, however, when I stepped into the foyer of the mansion.

I barely even remembered to step aside to allow room for Isaac and Gen to cross over the threshold.

I could almost begin to understand why Leo had referred to the mansion as humble. It wasn't because the inside was underwhelming, but, ironically, because it was quite the opposite. The grandeur of the interior made the outside, no matter how grand it at first appeared, feel like a cruel oversimplification.

The towering structure with its empirical arching windows did not do any justice to the monumental interior.

I found myself checking over my shoulder through the door just to make sure we were still in Gillonsville. I was almost surprised when it was proven to be true. I couldn't help but feel as if Connecticut didn't set a scene suggestive of the majestic sloping ceilings, or the elegantly curved railings.

Connecticut set a scene in my mind lending itself to the more subtle architecture so characteristic of the New

England. It was understated, eclectic, even. Nothing like this.

Connecticut didn't seem to fit the hardwood floors polished so meticulously that a fuzzy Kelsey gazed back at me when I adjusted my gaze to them. Nor did Connecticut seem to advocate for the crystal encrusted umbrella holder, or the intricately woven doormat.

The lavish interior of the mansion seemed to be more indicative of Beverly Hills, the type of city with a name so often preceded by "The Real Housewives of."

"So are you just going to stand there and gawk all day, or can we get down to business?"

Leo's voice reminded me there was something in the world besides his house, and the questions it raised.

"You have to admit," Isaac defended, "it is pretty awesome."

"I suppose so," Leo said, scanning the room, his face unimpressed. "But I'm used to it."

I almost felt sad. To me, a life so luxurious that one no longer appreciates remarkable things isn't really much of a life worth living. I hope I never get so used to beautiful things that they no longer appear beautiful. "So if you don't think this qualifies as amazing, what does?"

Leo shrugged. "A good beer, a cigarette bummed from a good friend, the simpler things. When you spend your life surrounded by stuff like this," he said, gesturing to some art which made even the air surrounding it feel expensive, "it's the little things that are amazing. Sometimes a life like this makes the expected the unexpected." He ended the conversation by departing down a expansive hallway, motioning for us to follow.

After navigating through the kitchen and a maze of doors so complex I felt the need to perhaps leave a bread-crumb trail, lest I ever want to make it back out, we emerged into the basement.

If any room was deserving of the title "Man Cave" it was this one. The carpet was plush and deep red, and a huge leather couch took up the greater part of one of the walls. The room was an unusual shape, a trapezoid with the hallway forming one of the diagonals. A deer's head was mounted above the polished pool table, entertaining a stereotype so decidedly that it was almost laughable.

Leo pulled a beer out of the refrigerator in the corner, and hold up three more. "Oh, no thanks," Gen denied quickly. "We're thirteen, remember?"

"I remembered," Leo said, the crack and hiss of his beer can opening fitting in neatly with his words. "I was just testing your morals."

"How'd we do?" Isaac said blandly.

"You have morals. Nicely done in general, but you failed in my book."

"Too bad for you," I deflected, absently picking up a pool ball and tossing it between my two hands.

A few seconds pause later, Leo thrust his hand in the direction of the pool table. "Rack them up. You know the stakes. You three versus me."

I removed the wooden triangle from around the pyr-amid of striped and solid balls, moving to place the cue ball on the other end of the table. "Want to break them?" I said, making eye contact with Leo, who had abandoned his leather jacket, revealing an equally black t-shirt.

The second he lined up his first shot, my heart sank. His victory seemed all but inevitable. He held the cue like he was born with it in his hands, and when he shot the pyramid dispersed perfectly, splaying the balls evenly across the green felt terrain. A blue ball dropped into the far corner pocket, and an orange one followed suit, rolling smoothly into one of the side pockets.

"You do this a lot, then?" Gen said. Her statement could have sounded impressed, but her expression told a different story, a story the same as mine. She was terrified.

"You could say so. It's easier now though." He lined up another shot. A purple ball stopped short of the right center. "Dammit."

"Easier now as opposed to when?" I lined up my first shot, knowing I wasn't making it look nearly as easy as Leo did. By some miracle, a yellow striped ball dropped into the corner pocket.

"I take it you don't make shots a lot?" Leo said, his face smug as I lined up my next shot. "Anyways, I mean easier as opposed to when I had to stand on an apple box to reach the table."

"You've been playing that long?" I said, incredulous. "Crap. Scratch."

"You bet," Leo affirmed. He lined up again, and sunk another two balls before missing. With every ball, I felt a deeper sense of doom. "Gen, you're up."

Gen shot me a secret smile, one which, for a strange reason, quelled my panic. She lined up and dropped two balls into the corner pocket.

"Damn, you're good," Leo affirmed, rubbing his chin.

Gen waved her hand dismissively. "Country club kid. The adults drink, and the kids golf and play pool. You should see me with a putter."

One ball later, Gen missed. Leo lined up for his turn, and succeeded for three goes until his luck ran out.

I ran a hand through my hair as I watched him. When he missed, I was taken aback. It almost looked as though he had set up the shot incorrectly on purpose. I pushed the thought out of my mind. There was no way.

The tension continued until every ball but the eight had found a home.

"Eight ball, corner pocket," Leo declared, draining the last sip of his beer.

Leo leaned over the side of the green, and positioned the cue on top of his hand. His shot happened in slow motion. The cue slid between his fingers, then, at the last moment, jerked to the left. He missed the ball entirely.

The same feeling as before hit me in the gut. *He couldn't be failing on purpose, could he?*

He simply shrugged, and gestured to Gen. "Eight ball, side pocket," she declared, although her voice shook.

I didn't dare breathe as she adjusted for the shot. I could see her tracing the angles in her mind. I knew there would be no luck in her shot, only success or errors in calculation. She pulled back and shot.

The eight ball dropped into the pocket. Relief flooded me as I breathed deeply, but before I could celebrate, Gen was already turning to Leo.

"A deal's a deal. Tell us what you know."

Leo didn't even appear surprised. My mouth felt dry. He pointed to the couch. "Sit. I'll talk."

The couch was L shaped. Isaac, Gen, and I occupied the longer two thirds, and Leo sat diagonal to us on the shorter end. Despite the plush nature of the brown leather couch, I sat toward the edge, sitting up stick-straight.

Gen spoke first. "Start basic. You immediately reacted when we mentioned Peter Montague. So what does that name mean to you?"

"No getting past you, huh?"

"No, there isn't."

Leo's tone had been light, which I had quickly calculated as a faux-paus. Gen would not deal with levity when she entered this mode of intensity.

Leo held his hands up, palms forward. "Okay. Point taken. Peter Montague..." Leo paused.

"Don't hide anything," Gen said quickly.

Something darker flashed in Leo's eyes. "I'm thinking. Would you rather I forgot something?"

Gen looked at her shoes.

"*Alright*," Leo continued. "When I was younger, my dad worked with Montague." *So he was the rogue apprentice,* my mind screamed. "He would talk about it at the dinner table. Proud, almost, or at least that's how it seemed. He would work long days, and he'd come home dressed all weird. Like Isaac is now, actually."

Isaac frowned, rubbing his hands on his pantaloons as though it could dispel the plaid.

"Then, one day, he came home, and it wasn't the same. This was several months ago. He was angry. And when my father gets angry…" Leo trailed off, absently rubbing his cheek.

"Did he…"

"Still answering your first question, Junior. So I ask my dad what's wrong. He starts ranting. Yelling about restrictions, trust. I've never seen him that mad. He didn't go to work the next day. Or the day after that. Or any day, really. Then, a week ago, he comes downstairs, dressed in the strange clothes again. He had this strange look in his eyes. When he came home, he seemed satisfied. I asked him why, but…"

"But, what?" Gen said, eyes wide.

"His answer didn't make any sense."

"What did he say?" Gen pressed.

"He said, 'he's not a problem anymore.'"

It felt as though someone had slid an ice cube down the back of my dress. I shivered involuntarily, curling my toes inside of my shoes.

"I knew immediately that 'he' was Peter, but it took me longer to figure out what my father had done."

"He didn't kill him, did he?" I blurted.

"Well, that's what I thought at first," Leo admitted. "But, no. My dad's a proud guy. It didn't take much for me to find out what happened. He said he 'had' Peter. I assumed it was a kidnapping sort of situation. So, boom," Leo said, sounding almost wistful. "Just like that, the man who used to take me to baseball games is a felon. Great."

I couldn't keep a image of a younger Leo's messy black hair crammed into a baseball cap –hotdog in one hand, soda in the other– from popping into my head. I saw his point.

Leo blinked a few times, then pushed his hair back where it had gotten stuck to his forehead by a combination of gel and sweat. "Well, if Peter was your mentor, when are you from?"

Gen glowered. "We won. You answer our questions, not the other way– Wait a second, did you say *when*? How do you know about *when*?"

"Oh, I must have misspoken," Leo said, sounding uncharacteristically nervous. "I meant where. Where are you from?"

"No," Gen said. "Don't turn this around. All you said was your dad left and came back, and that he was wearing strange clothes. How do you know about '*when*'?"

"It doesn't matter. It's too long of a story for right now, anyways."

"Leo," I said, "we're here for you to tell us long stories. Make this worth our time. You lost the bet. You talk. Those were the rules."

Leo stared at the ceiling for a painstakingly long amount of time. I was just beginning to fight the urge to kick him out of his trance when he finally looked back down. "Fine." He sat up straighter. "Fine. I know about when because my father told me about it. When he came home ranting, it wasn't nonsense. It was about power, and how Peter wouldn't give it to him. About how he was so close to understanding the watches. About how Peter told him he was too power hungry, and kicked him out. I still didn't understand completely, so I took matters into my own hands to find out."

Isaac spoke for the first time. "Sorry, what?"

"He wouldn't tell me the full story. I was frustrated. So one day, before the kidnapping, I broke into his office while he was sleeping. I found this journal. It had a title. *The Peculiar Habits of Watches,* or something like that."

"*The Watches and Their Peculiar Habits,*" Gen supplied, her voice barely a whisper.

Leo squinted at her appraisingly. "Yeah, that. How did you know?"

Gen simply shook her head. "What did you do with it?"

Leo laughed dryly. "It's a journal. I read it. What else would you do?"

"And you found?" I asked slowly.

"There was an entry…" Leo reached into his leather jacket, and pulled out a sheath of thoroughly crumpled paper.

I leaned toward it. The paper looked familiar in size. The edges were all torn, but the tears on one side looked fresh and deliberate. When I squinted, I could make out handwriting. *Why was it so familiar?* I felt a surge of adrenaline as I placed the familiarity. Black ink. Spindly lettering. Torn out pages. *Peter's journal.*

Gen reached for it, recognizing it as well, but Leo clutched it closer to his chest. "It's about my father."

"Why did you steal it?" Gen said.

I could see Leo's knuckles turning white as they gripped the aged paper. "I couldn't help myself." His face harbored a sort of innocent panic that looked foreign, almost ill-fitting. "It explains everything. It explains what he wanted. *The purple moon.* I'd heard him mention it before, but I had no idea what it meant."

I opened my mouth, but Gen grabbed my hand, and I quieted.

Leo gave me a strange look, but continued nevertheless. "You can read it, if you want. Just give it back when you're done."

When I met his eyes I felt oddly sympathetic. He looked like a baby, insecurely giving up his security blanket. At least, this was what I thought at first. When I looked closer, my heart jolted. I could have sworn, for a moment, that a shadow of something sinister crossed over him. I brushed it away, instead looking over Gen's shoulder when she look the paper. I remembered how the last entry ended... *He said he'd be back. He said that next time he'd come for more than just the purple-*. This was the second half of our puzzle, and I couldn't believe my eyes when I read it.

*-moon. He said he'd come for me. A part of me is skeptical. I always knew Rupert to be power hungry, but, to an extent, I believed that his ambition could be*

*kept in check. But something was different from the boy I once knew when he left the shop that day. He wasn't who I thought he was. It was a whole new kind of deception. He had not been in disguise. The hints had all been there. The way he constantly questioned me as I sent him back to 1952 each night, demanding to have control over his exits and returns. He would never accept what I asked of him, a sort of blind faith it was perhaps unfair to expect. But this was what seemed sensible. If I taught him the mechanics before he was fully trained in the art, there would be no way to insure that he returned at all. This was my greatest fear. I suppose, on the most fundamental of levels, I am simply a fearful old man. Afraid of being alone... Although it is not so much that. I am afraid of the damage I could do to this world. I am as afraid of Erindale as I am of myself. When I took him in as my apprentice, I never could have imagined... Or maybe I could have, but I turned a blind eye as opposed to a weary one. Foolish.*

*Erindale has a boy. Leo. He talks about him sometimes. Sometimes I wonder if this is the only tenderness left in the man. The only person he feels a need to protect besides himself.*

I looked up at Leo before I continued reading. Something in his eyes told me he knew the lines I was digesting. Something told me these lines were the real reason he stole the pages.

*When he left, I told him it had to be for the last time. I told him I would send him back to 1952, without a way home. He left the shop before I could return him, as if in a flash, disappearing while I had my back turned. I can only assume he is still here, in 1811. I fear the day he returns.*

The last sentence of the entry pulled my lips into a frown. *So Peter knew he would come back?*

Gen looked up. "So he got stuck?"

Leo cleared his throat. "Yes… and looking at the date of the entry…" he trailed off.

Isaac frowned. "What?"

"It lines up perfectly with one of his bouts of absenteeism."

"Do you know how he got back?"

"No," the younger Erindale said absently. "I never could figure that one out."

"Okay," Gen said, suspicion edging into the corners of her tone. "Where are they now?"

"Well that was blunt. Where's the interrogation light? The good cop-bad cop? Oh, hold on, I need to grab my handcuffs so you can strap me to the table." His joking tone was cut with thinly veiled discomfort.

Gen sighed. "Leo, it's late. Answer the question."

"To the best of my knowledge, the watchmaker's."

"What makes you think that?"

"Look, Gen," Leo said, tousling his hair. "Not everything has a fascinating backstory. That's just what I know."

I saw Gen hesitate to accept the answer. Her eyes flashed from side to side, but eventually settled. "Alright. The watchmaker's. Has he been staying there, or has he been coming home?"

"Staying," Leo said softly. "Not exactly interested in this place anymore. Not when he has power at his disposal."

The air was filled with a loaded silence. Finally: "Any other questions?" Leo fell back into the cushions, which moved to cradle his form.

"Why tell us all this?" I said, after another painfully long pause.

Leo shrugged. "You won."

"Leo, this isn't about a simple game of pool," Gen interjected.

"That wasn't what I meant."

Before I could ask about his cryptic statement, Leo was on his feet. He walked back towards the pool table, running his hand along the perimeter. "Where are you staying tonight?"

Gen looked at me, then at Leo. "We don't exactly know. We were making our plan when we saw you at Kelly's, and now..."

Leo paused, resting his hand on the table. He picked up a ball and rolled it between his palms. His silence lasted for an uncomfortably long span of time. I could hear the hum of the light bulbs illuminating the room, my mind desperately latching on to any sound it could find in the silence. He set down the ball. "My dad shouldn't come home tonight."

"And?" Gen said. The circles ever-present under her eyes had deepened. She rubbed at them with the heels of her hands.

"And, you can stay here if you want, I suppose."

"Seriously?" Isaac said. "What's your motive?"

Leo's laugh was harsh. "Can't I just be nice?"

"You're the son of our enemy," Gen said bluntly. "Forgive us if we don't blindly believe you."

Leo frowned. "I'm his son, not him. Please do your best to avoid confusing those two things. I am *not* my father." He looked away, and when he turned back his nonchalant nature had returned. "I'll be upstairs, getting a room ready for you three. Take it or leave it."

Without another word, Leo was bounding up the stairs out of the basement, leaving us on the couch trapped within yet another distressing bout of silence.

"We can't stay here," Isaac said plainly, as soon as Leo's footsteps were out of earshot.

"Wait, why don't we trust him?" I cut in. "He really didn't seem like he was lying."

"Maybe not," Isaac said, "but I still think we're being dangerously naive if we ignore the fact he could be. I mean, come on Kels. It's his dad."

I bit my lip. "Yeah. I guess my thought is if we go questioning every little thing he tells us to do, we're going to move a lot slower."

"And, on that note," Gen remarked, "if we leave tonight, it shows we don't trust him. I still think he knows more than he let on to in the first place. We need to get that information from him before we dare get on his bad side.

"But why would he hold anything back at all?" Isaac reasoned. "If he was truly trustworthy he would have told us everything from the get-go."

Gen twisted her watch around her wrist, tracing her finger over the fleur-de-lis. "We can't lose him, Isaac. He's the best lead we've got."

"I'd rather lose him than destroy our chance of success."

"He *is* our chance of success!" Gen argued. "What happens if we leave him now? He'll go to Rupert and tell him everything he knows about us, everything we're trying to do. Can we risk that?"

"We can't avoid taking risks," I added, looking at Isaac pointedly.

Gen frowned. "We can't avoid risks altogether, Isaac. We only need to be wise enough to not be reckless, but brave enough to take great risks."

"Frank Warren," Isaac muttered.

"What?" Gen said, exasperated.

"That's a Frank Warren quote." When Gen continued to stare back at him blankly, Isaac added, "His TEDTalk was viewed more than two million times." Isaac shrugged. "Sometimes I know things."

There was a long pause.

"How do you judge if a risk is worth taking?" Isaac finally said, softly. "I'm just worried about you two. I want you safe."

"Well, that's what makes it a risk, isn't it?" I said. Deep breath. In. One, two, three. Out. One, two, three. "When it comes down to it, every single action we take is a risk. That's what we signed up for when we took on this adventure. Everything we've done since we've left 2018 has been a risk, like it or not. The question is where the line dividing reasonable risks and unreasonable risks is." In. One, two, three. Out. One, two, three. "But I think the line is wherever you want to put it. It's more a matter of what you're willing to do to make what you want happen. But if you don't want to take any risks, then you don't want to live."

Isaac stared at his lap. "You sound like Gen."

"But am I wrong?"

Isaac sighed. "No, you aren't." He smirked. "That's why you sound like Gen."

Gen stopped twisting her watch. "So we're staying."

Isaac nodded hesitantly. "I don't know what else to do. You two are right. We can't risk losing Leo, so if this is the way…"

We sat quietly.

I looked around the room. The pool table, the couch… all the elements of the room were so innocent. Not designed for the weight of the situations they had just managed. When I listened closely, I could have sworn I heard Leo talking upstairs. I ran the fabric of my dress between my fingers. *It's your imagination. Be brave, Kelsey.* I swallowed hard, and released the cloth.

A few moments later, Leo reentered the basement. "Staying?"

We nodded. Leo pointed up the stairs, a wide grin spreading across his face. "Bedtime, then."

The room he lead us to was as grand as the rest of the house. The bed was a four poster made of white wood, although it had no canopy. Beside that, there was a gray cloth futon. The room was carpeted in a matching gray, and the walls were thoroughly coated with paintings. Gen and I shared the queen bed, and Isaac curled up on the futon almost immediately, clicking the standing lamp off.

I can't remember the exact moment I crossed the threshold between conscience and sleep. All I remember is the soft sounds of Isaac and Gen's breath fading into silence as I slipped away. And, in that moment, their presence was enough.

# CHAPTER SIXTEEN

I woke up to see Gen and Isaac still sound asleep beside me. Gen's hair criss-crossed her face, and lines were pressed deep into Isaac's face where it had been squished into his pillows. I carefully pulled aside the comforter and climbed out of bed, smoothing it back down to cover Gen completely.

I wished for socks as the cold floor made contact with my bare toes. I sat back down on the edge of the bed for a moment, staring at a small red alarm clock positioned on the side table. *6:34 am.*

I rubbed at my eyes with tight fists. Finally, I stood once more and made for the door. My hand had just closed around the cool metal of the knob when I paused, hearing a soft voice in the hallway.

*No, father, they're not awake yet.* The voice paused. *I don't think I can move them without waking them up.* Another pause, this one longer. *I already told you everything they told me.* Pause.

*What does it matter what I told them?* The next pause was barely a breath's length. *No, I didn't lie! Why would I if this was our plan?* Pause. *Yes, and I'm sorry but– No, no, I understand. It's okay, I know how to trap them.*

Trap them… I clasped my hand over my mouth, stifling an inadvertent yelp. *Leo.*

It couldn't be. I pressed my ear closer to the door, removing my hand from the knob.

*So when they wake up, then?* Pause. *Okay, I'll check now. I'll be right back.*

My breath hitched in my throat. Footsteps, coming toward the door.

I scrambled back toward the bed, throwing myself back under the covers. I scrunched my eyes tight, and threw my arm over my head, trying my best to look as though I had been sleeping. I had barely stopped moving when I heard the door open.

Heavy breathing paused in the entryway for a long moment. I curled my toes under the covers, trying to stifle the urge to fidget.

The breathing retreated. The second I heard the door close, I scampered back to the wall, pressing my ear against it once more.

*All still asleep.* Leo sounded almost satisfied. The betrayal left a bitter taste on my tongue.

His voice sounded scrambled through the door, like a Bond villain's. Everything in me wanted to pretend it belonged to someone besides him, but I knew better. It had that same undertone.

*I'll keep an eye on them.*

My skin itched with Leo's final admission.

*Alright. Okay. See you later dad. Goodbye.*

My head whirled. Something in me managed to lock the door before I stumbled back to the bed, sliding down against the frame at the foot. My heart ached and pounded all at the same time. *He tricked us.* The thought was quickly replaced with a new, burning question. *Did we trick ourselves?* After all, maybe it was insane to believe that we could trust Leo at all. It was the little things I had let slide. His awkward pauses when he spoke. The talking upstairs when he said he was preparing our room.

That had been another phone call, I was almost certain of it. I was fuming. My face burned, and I couldn't decide if it was out of embarrassment or pure anger. Probably some compound of both.

I struggled to rein in my thoughts. *Now.* What do we do *now*? Could we time travel to get away? I stared at my watch for a long moment, before scrapping the idea. Without the raw stones, we were still hopeless.

*What else, what else?* my mind screamed. He said he was waiting for us to wake up, so… I looked at Isaac and Gen's forms, still curled up, blissfully unaware. Isaac's mouth hung slightly open, his breath pushing stray hairs out of his face. His glasses were folded around the collar of his shirt. He looked painfully peaceful.

I didn't want to break their illusion. I didn't want to tell them. But I had to. It didn't take the ticking of my watch to remind me that we were running out of time. All it would take was a squeaky floorboard or an uncontrolled sneeze to alert Leo of our wakefulness. I didn't know what his exact plan was, but his tone told me I didn't want to be on the receiving end of it.

I wanted to talk to Gen. She was the master planner, not me. This wasn't my domain. But, despite this, I knew better than to wake her. Our voices, however whispering, could not be trusted. For all we knew, Leo could be right outside the door. I had to make this plan alone.

I tried to peer under the crack. The cold floor pulled some of the redness from my cheeks, but I could discern nothing from the shadowy line.

I sat back up, and twisted my hair back into a knot. *Think.* Erindale wants us with him. So, logically, Leo's instructions would be to take us to the watchmaker's. "*And what is the last thing he'd expect us to do?*" Gen's voice questioned in my head.

"Just that," I whispered.

I looked around the room, taking inventory. *Bedsheets. A window.* I counted the sheets. Gen's, Isaac's, and the fitted sheet from the bed. *We're on the second floor?* The sheets formed a rope in my mind. It would be risky. We'd probably still have to drop a few feet to the ground. But it was the best –and only– plan I had.

It would have to do.

When I woke up Gen, it was with my hand pressed over her mouth. Her eyes went wide with fear for a long moment, before they relaxed with the recognition of my face. I leaned close to her ear, removing my hand.

"Leo betrayed us." I didn't dare allow my voice to breach a whisper.

"WHA–" I clapped my hand back over her mouth.

"I heard him on the phone with Rupert," I whispered. I silenced as I heard a shift in the boards from the hallway. When I spoke again, my voice was even lower. "Leo is waiting for us to wake up. He has a plan for when we do." I saw a question in Gen's dark brown eyes. "I don't know what it is," I answered. "We need to be quiet. Start knotting your sheet while I wake up Isaac."

Her brow creased.

"Just trust me. Follow my lead."

Despite her visible confusion, she sat up and began knotting.

I tiptoed over to Isaac, doing my best to avoid creaking the boards. I followed the same procedure as I had with Gen, placing my hand over his mouth before I gently roused him. He jolted when he woke, desperately trying to break free from my grasp.

"Isaac, no," I hissed through gritted teeth. "I'm going to move my hand, but you have to listen."

I told him what I told Gen, and by the end of my miniature speech his eyes were as wide as dinner plates.

Finally, he broke his trance, his lips twitching into the slightest of smirks. "I suppose now would be a bad time to say I told you so?" His words were feather light.

I punched him gently in the shoulder. "Yes," I whispered

back, although I secretly appreciated his attempts at relief. "Now, listen to me. I need you to take your sheet, and knot it. When you're done, bring it to me."

He glanced nervously at the window. "Kelsey, if we fall..."

Although I was still whispering, my tone was firm. "Do you have a different plan?"

He silently began to knot the sheet. I listened for a moment, then pulled the fitted sheet out from underneath of Gen.

I began tying thick knots in the cloth, placing about a foot between each. My hands shook as I tied each knot. The rhythmic motion did nothing to sooth me, and my mind was overwhelmed with doubt.

*What if I was setting us up for disaster? What if the sheets didn't hold?* I tried to stifle the feelings but it came to no avail. Finally, after minutes which had imitated hours, I finished the sheet.

Isaac and Gen stood in front of me, holding out sheets of their own. Together we tied final knots connecting them at the ends.

I moved toward the window, after tying the makeshift rope to the bed, positioning my hands against the frame.

I turned back to face my friends. "If this is loud, we have to move quickly. I locked the door, but Leo will get in anyways. When we get to the bottom, start running down the street. We'll meet two blocks away."

Isaac's face was soft. "You two go first," he whispered. "If Leo gets one of us, I want it to be me."

I took my hands off of the frame. "Isaac, you can't–"

He grabbed my arm. "Yes, I can. And I will. If he gets me, you know he'll take me to the watchmaker's. Just..." his voice fell short.

"Just, what?" I asked quietly.

"Just come get me," he said, smiling ever so slightly.

Gen and I nodded. Then, in an instant, we were all wrapped in each others arms. My throat felt tight, but I managed to push four words through the pinhole opening. "I love you two."

When we separated, I rubbed at my eyes for a moment. "Let's do this," I whispered, pulling confidence back into my tone.

I reached for the window once more. *Three. Two. One.* I thrust the frame upward, and the sound was monumental.

Almost instantly, the doorknob began to rattle.

Gen was first out, sliding down the rope quickly. I heard only a soft thud when she hit the ground.

The doorknob rattled again, this time with even stronger ferocity. "Kelsey, go!" Isaac demanded.

My heart tore in two as I swung my leg out of the window, shimmying down the rope. When my shoes hit the grass, I couldn't help but look back before I began to run.

One of Isaac's legs was through the window.

Reassurance flooded me, and I took off.

My footsteps slowed when I saw Gen on the corner two blocks away, bent against a rusting lamp post.

I turned around before I even acknowledged her.

*Isaac. Isaac. Isaac.* His name was a mantra in my mind. I squinted down the streets.

"Kels," Gen said hesitantly. "Where is he?"

I felt my legs turn to jello beneath me, and when I turned back to her it was with all-too wet eyes. "I don't know."

Gen's breathing leveled out before mine. "Okay. Let's be rational. If Leo took Isaac, it would be to the watchmaker's. Just like Isaac said."

"Gen, how can you be calm?" I couldn't keep the hysteria out of my tone. "He *took* Isaac."

Gen clasped two hands on my shoulders. "Kelsey. Breathe. We made a plan."

I couldn't stop my breath from hitching. "But what if he does something to him before we get there."

Tears. Tears poured down my face, carving rivers down my pale cheeks. Somewhere, I was sure, at the smallest atomic level, my fears were spelled out within the molecules. Somewhere, each proton, neutron, and electron spelled out the words which threatened to explode me.

"He won't," Gen reassured, although it sounded painfully half-hearted.

I scrubbed at my eyes. The salt burned my hands where they had scraped when I fell. "Gen, you know that's not guaranteed."

Gen looked at the sky for a moment, then turned back down to meet my eyes. "It's not. You're right. I'm not going to try to tell you that Isaac is undoubtedly safe, because, quite frankly, he probably isn't. But he's counting on us to save him, and standing here isn't doing that."

I swallowed the lump in my throat once and for all, burying it deep down where it couldn't affect me. "To the watchmaker's, then."

Gen nodded. "To the watchmaker's."

# CHAPTER SEVENTEEN

It only took us a few moments to orient ourselves before we began our trek back toward Main Street. The sights of the streets that had once enthralled me now seemed dull despite the best efforts of their bright pastel tones. Now it seemed almost rude, the way in which the attitudes of the streets failed to match the fear settled within me.

Isaac's face was a relentless constant in my mind. I imagined how it must have happened.

His leg, the one which I had seen, would have been pulled back through the window frame. How did he feel when Leo grabbed him? I both desperately did and didn't want to know. What did Leo say? This was the question which hurt me the most.

Isaac was not the type to take words lightly.

My shoulder collided with a tree, jolting me from my thoughts.

"Kelsey, watch where you're going!"

"Huh?" My voice sounded bleary.

"Focus! Have you been listening to a word I've said?"

I frowned deeply. "No, I'm sorry, Gen. I just..." The fabric of my dress found its way into my hands once more.

Gen placed her hand on my shoulder. "I know. It's okay. Listen now."

"Okay."

Gen quickened her pace. I hadn't noticed her slowing down. "So when we get there, there are two possible scenarios. One–" she held up a finger "–Erindale isn't in the main shop, and we can sneak in ourselves. If we do that, we have the element of surprise on our side."

"And if not?"

"That's option two. We let him take us. Odds are he'll take us straight to Isaac and Peter, in that case. Then, we can figure out what all of this has been about right away."

I nodded once more, feeling almost like a soldier. My orders were assigned. Now it was time to do my duties, and to do them without hesitation. "Either way, our priorities are Isaac and Peter," I added. "Rupert is secondary. If we can find a way to take care of him, great. But I'm more worried about those two."

Gen made a small noise of consent.

The walk to main street had taken all of thirty minutes, but it had felt like hours longer. If Isaac and Leo had driven or taken a cab they would be wildly ahead of us.

Twenty minutes didn't seem like all that much, but as I stared at the facade of the watchmaker's... Well, it could suffice to say that twenty minutes felt like nothing shy of an eternity.

An eternity to do whatever Rupert and Leo pleased to Peter, to Isaac.

Looking upon it now, there was a part of me which almost wished that we had confronted Rupert as soon as we arrived. As much as I knew it would have been a lost cause, it seemed almost worth it to quell the pain our separation from Isaac was now causing.

Gen stepped up to the door, and touched the knob tentatively. She clasped it tighter, and twisted. It rotated, and Gen looked back to me, relief flooding her features.

She eased the door open slowly, cringing as the hinges gave way with a feeble whine. Her body slid through the small crack in the door almost seamlessly, and I followed, closing it gently behind me.

The store was dark, the only light that which filtered in from the high windows on the front wall. I could see the shadow of Gen's hand in the dark, and it motioned me to follow her out of the shop.

When we reached the hallway, Gen paused, peering down either end. Her hand gestured once more, and I followed.

A few feet into her right turn, I recognized that she was making for Peter's room.

Every footfall felt prenaturally loud, and I winced as we crept down the hall.

A few of the lamps dotting the walls had been lit, but the hallway still remained largely in shadow.

I could see Peter's door. Without remembering it perfectly, I am almost certain that I saw Gen's hand reaching for the knob when the shadow appeared behind me.

I smacked my hand over my mouth, trying to stifle my scream.

It was not silenced enough for Gen, who quickly looked back at me.

Her face matched what I imagined mine to be. She grabbed my arm, and pointed for me to turn around. When I did, my terror doubled in size.

*Harvey. Harvey.* His name was like a broken record spiraling through my mind. The record scratched and changed its tune. A man from almost a century before. A man with a cane and a broken watch and broken morals. The man who gave us the poem that took us here.

"Harvey." I couldn't stop the word from falling from my lips. "Are you working with him?"

Harvey laughed. "*Harvey?* How dense are you? Have you really not figured it out?" He gave a sharp tug on Gen and I, pulling us toward him. "Either way, follow me, and if you try to run away…" He paused dramatically, his fleshy fingers gripping my arm tighter through the cloth of my dress. "*I'll shoot you.*" He let go of her for a split second to pull aside his tweed jacket, revealing a pistol. "Follow me," Harvey said once more. "And *don't* call me Harvey."

"Why not?" Gen said. She pulled her arm free, but still walked after him.

"Because it's not my name, junior."

Something clicked in my head. It was going out on an insane limb, but... No, it couldn't be. It was a perfectly common expression. Leo's voice echoed in my mind. *Junior,* he had said.

"Rupert Erindale," I said, not daring to raise my voice.

"Ding ding ding! We have a winner!" Harvey– no, Rupert– exclaimed. He exited the elevator, then turned, pressing a hand to his chest. "What gave me away?"

I bit my lip until I tasted blood.

"So you're Rupert... and Harvey?" Gen spoke slower than I'd ever heard her, clearly struggling to understand. "I don't understand."

Rupert frowned. "Now Peter told me that you all were meant to be intelligent. Don't you get it? Harvey was never real." His voice turned mocking. "*Oh, my watch is broken! Oh, can't you fix it?* Don't you get it? I planted that poem! It was *always* me."

"What?" Gen gasped. "But why would you give that to us?"

"Where are Isaac and Peter?" I added, practically talking over Gen.

"My god," Rupert deflected. "Do you two do anything but ask questions? I saw something flicker through his eyes, but it was gone before I could read it. "Do you think this is a game? That I'm just going to tell you my plans to give you an advantage?"

"You're the one with the gun," Gen boldly pointed out. "Therefore I may suggest you have the advantage right now."

Rupert's hand brushed where the weapon was concealed by his jacket. "Yes," he agreed, "I have the upper hand here. I am in control. And it would be in your best interest to remember that."

I fought the urge to tell him exactly where he could put his "upper hand."

I gritted my teeth. "Where are they? I won't say a word until we're back with them."

Rupert breathed out an exaggerated sigh. "Are all teenagers this unbearable?"

"Take us to them."

Rupert locked eyes with me. My heart pounded, but somehow, something within me managed to maintain eye contact. He stared for a few seconds longer, and I could sense Gen's panic behind me. "Fine," he said finally. "You want to be taken to them, I'll do it. Alone or together, it'll be the same fate."

Rupert led us into the kitchen of the watchmaker's and my heart sank even deeper when I saw Isaac and Peter.

Isaac's eyes shone with barely subdued panic from where he sat stick straight in one of the large wooden chairs. His hair was wild, and his pants were torn on one leg. I winced as I realized the tear's probable origins. I couldn't help but realize how wrong it was that despite all of this I felt relieved. He was breathing. That had become the standard.

Then there was Peter, in the chair right next to Isaac's. His glasses were askew on his face, one side of them cracked enough for me to fear a shard of glass would bridge the gap into his eye. His shirt was ripped. I couldn't tell if it was the product of tearing hands or a knife.

Crimson trailed down his clothing in a long stain, probably about two days old, and I prayed for a nosebleed, not internal bleeding. The extent to which he was stooped over and the hand pressed into his stomach, however, didn't give me much hope for such profitable outcomes.

When we first met Peter, despite his elderly presentation, I thought of him as an untouchable wizard, a powerhouse, controlling the very air he inhabited. Looking at him now, though, I found myself thinking the most he could control was probably an ant.

It was unsettling in an uncomfortably deep way, to see someone who I saw as so strong become so weak. Despite the general aura of sadness Peter carried, he smiled when he saw us. It pulled at the dried blood on his face until it cracked apart.

I looked to the corner of the room as I heard a small cough. My blood boiled. *Leo.* Leaned against the wall, stupid leather jacket tucked around his form. His face was unbearably smug. Red edged into the corners of my vision as I looked at him. *How dare he?* I clenched my hands at my sides, doing my best to avoid showing my frustration. I wouldn't give him the satisfaction. As I stared I noticed something strange in his expression. Something almost apologetic.

I felt my stomach flip violently, and I forced myself to look away. "Peter," I said instead.

"Kelsey, Gen," he acknowledged weakly. His smile grew wider. "I knew you three could do it."

I stepped closer to Peter. "Peter, I don't understand. Did you know–"

"Enough!" Rupert said sharply, grabbing my clothes to yank me back. His tone was not mocking as it had been before. Now it was merely dark. "This is not what we are here to do."

"Then what are we here to do," Gen said. "Because as of now it seems like we're not accomplishing anything." She tilted her chin upward, meeting Rupert's eyes.

I noticed that she, too, avoided looking at Leo.

"I'm so thrilled that you would ask, Genevieve," Rupert replied. He drew two chairs away from the table, placing them next to Isaac and Peter. He shoved me and Gen into them, then stared at us appraisingly.

His lilting demeanor was back when he spoke again. "Consider it a bit of a… Russian roulette. I will ask you questions, and you will take turns answering them. Each answer given keeps you alive for another round. Failure to answer will be on a three strike system."

He began to pace around the room, his brown loafers echoing against the stone. "First unanswered question, and I will give you a sample of what I can do to you." He cracked his knuckles.

Isaac looked at me with a confused squint, and I stared back with barely controlled distress.

"Second unanswered question," Rupert continued, "I will *make sure* you know what I can do to you." This time he flashed a small silver blade, not unlike the one Gen used to cut apart the brick wall on the night it all began.

"And the third?" I asked. I cursed my voice for shaking.

A devilish grin crept across Rupert's vaguely stubbly face. He reached into his waistband and produced the gun. "Take a guess."

"What if we run?" Gen asked.

Rupert's grin appeared to expand impossibly wider. "You're out."

I could feel my hands beginning to shake, so I shoved them under my legs, squashing them against the seat of the chair.

"We don't know anything!" Gen blurted out in protest.

Rupert squatted down in front of her, uncomfortably close. "That is a lie, little girl. If you knew nothing, you wouldn't be here. You figured out the poem. There's no other way."

"I still don't understand," Gen replied. "Why would you give us the poem if it would only lead us to what you wanted? Why not just find it yourself?"

Rupert turned to Peter with an exaggerated sigh. "Why are they *so* dull? You go on and on about their intelligence–" I felt a surge of pride "–and yet they can't discern the simple and clear reason I would act the way I did."

Peter frowned deeply, and turned to us. "He gave it to you because he couldn't figure it out."

Gen's mouth gaped open. "What?"

"The location of the purple moon is written in the form of a poem so only those intelligent enough to wield its power are capable of finding it." Peter looked to Rupert pointedly at this. "I gave it to Rupert in the first place because I didn't see the harm. I knew he couldn't discern its meaning. He knew this, though. That was the problem."

"What do you mean?" I asked.

Rupert regained the stage. "Peter was right. I couldn't figure it out. But when he spoke of you three it was clear that he considered you far more capable. His 'superior apprentices.'"

*He* was *the rouge apprentice,* I thought. *We were right.*

"So I created Harvey. I hid the poem in the watch, knowing you would open it. Then I came, and gave it up. After that, it was merely a waiting game. I knew you would come when you found it. Thirteen-year-olds. Hopelessly sentimental."

Isaac rubbed his hands on his pants. "But why would you want us here?"

"Because you know where the purple moon is. Now, you can tell me, and it will be mine."

"Give us a single reason we should tell you," Gen said firmly.

Rupert's hand ghosted over the gun, which he had set aside on the kitchen table. "Don't you remember our arrangement? You have to answer my questions. So, question number one…"

He leaned forward, close enough that I could smell his breath. It was foul. I glanced over his shoulder at Leo, whose expression remained unchanged.

"Where is it?"

# CHAPTER EIGHTEEN

"I'll tell you!" Gen blurted.

Alarm bells sounded in my head. "Gen!"

"No, Kelsey. We have to tell him." She looked up at Rupert as he moved to stand in front of her. He knelt down.

I saw Gen's throat move as she swallowed hard. "It's in the storefront. Behind the shelf next to the desk. It's on hinges, but it's pretty heavy." She glanced at Leo. "You should probably take him with you."

Warm relief surged through me, although it was combined with icy fear. I hoped Gen had a plan. Otherwise, when Erindale found out we were lying…

The eldest Erindale stood, joints popping as he rose. "Are you telling the truth?"

Gen nodded hard. "Yes." She feigned anxiety. "We told you, right? So now you won't hurt us. That was the deal."

Rupert nodded slowly. "If it's the truth. I don't think I need to remind you what the outcome will be should you have lied."

He gestured sharply to Leo, who moved away from the wall, walking toward his father. His footsteps sounded hollow against the floor.

"I'll be back," Rupert declared. He turned sharply on his heel and began to stride away.

I listened carefully as they walked down the hallway. As soon as I felt sure they had made a full retreat, I turned to Gen.

"Please tell me you know what you're doing."

"Of course I do," Gen said, tucking her hair behind her ears. "But if you want it to work, you need to focus. Isaac, too."

Isaac nodded obediently.

"We don't have very much time before he figures out that we lied, so we have to move quickly. If one of us can get to the purple moon and grab two of the pieces, we can use it to defeat them."

I was stupefied. "How?"

"Kelsey, we know how the purple moon works. All we have to do is get Rupert and Leo to think of a time that isn't this one. Then, get them to touch the pieces, and when they do they'll be sent there. Away from us."

"Why can't we just go?" I questioned.

Gen rolled her eyes. "*We* need to stay together. It's too risky. What if we think one year differently then can't catch up? That's a weakness. A weakness that it would be great to give to them."

"Gen, you're forgetting the risk," Isaac said nervously. "Last time we touched them we got sent here. There's no way to guarantee we won't end up time travelling again. And, beyond that, we're not really trapping them if they still have the purple moon."

"No, Isaac," Peter interjected, "Gen's right. It's the best option we have. The purple moons only work once, unless they're in the watches. They won't be able to go anywhere."

"But we still don't know that when we retrieve the stones to bring them in here, we won't be sent to another time." Isaac met Gen's eyes, still somewhat pleading.

"If we don't think of anytime but now, we'll stay here," Gen finished. "We have to take the risk. I'm willing to do it."

"No!" I exclaimed, surprising even myself. "I want to do this. I have to do this."

"Kelsey, that's insane, you can't–"

"No, Gen. I won't let you two go. I'd rather have something happen to me than..." I looked into her eyes, trying to nonverbally express the words I was too afraid to say.

Gen stared at me for a long moment, almost unblinking. "Okay. Okay. If you feel like you have to do it, do it. But *please* be careful."

I smiled as confidently as I could muster, although I knew it was unconvincing. "I will, Gen. Don't worry about me."

"No chance," Gen said, smiling weakly back.

I stood, beginning to walk away, but I was stopped by Peter's voice behind me.

"Be strong, Kelsey. You've made it this far."

His words gave me a new wave of confidence, which I allowed to push me through the door and into the hallway.

I held my breath as I tiptoed toward Peter's room. The hallway felt as though it were a mile long as I moved quickly but quietly through it. I stopped moving as I heard Leo's voice echoing from the storefront. "Is this the right shelf?"

I scampered as fast as I could through the rest of the hallway, finally allowing myself to breathe as I reached Peter's room. I gently closed the door and slid the lock into place. Safe, at least relatively.

I collapsed onto the floor beside the two o' clock board. My hands shook as I pulled each pin out of the wood. When they were all free, I slid the board aside.

The purple moons glowed with a sort of excitable energy. I breathed a sigh of relief, although it was cut short as I remembered the task at hand.

I cleared my head, looking around the room. *Here. Now. I only want to be right here, right now.* The phrases repeated in my mind until it was all I could think of. *Here. Now. I only want to be right here, right now. Here. Now. I only want to be right here, right now.*

I took a deep breath then reached down, picking up two of the pieces. They were cool in my hand. *Here. Now. I only want to be right here, right now. Here. Now. I only want to be right here, right now.* I stood slowly. *Here. Now. I only want to be right here, right now.* I folded the pieces into the fabric of my dress. The glow was visible through the cotton, albeit somewhat stifled. *Here. Now. I only want to be right here, right now.*

I held on to the cloth wrapped pieces with one hand, and opened the door with the other. The small crack I had created was just wide enough to peer through.

I held my breath as I saw Rupert and Leo exit the storefront. If it weren't for their all too apparent rage, I would have feared they might have noticed me.

*Here. Now. I only want to be right here, right now.*

As soon as they slid back into the kitchen, I opened the door the rest of the way and stepped back into the hall.

The pieces had begun to feel almost warm. Those pieces… I never could have anticipated that a small, purple fleur-de-lis was only the tip of the iceberg. When I first saw the watches in 2018 I was instantly enamoured– *No!* My mind screamed in protest. *No thinking of home. Here. Now. I only want to be right here, right now.*

The hallway felt unbearably cold as I walked back toward the kitchen, but despite this I could feel my palm sweating against the small, crescent stones.

"Where is she?" Rupert's voice boomed from the kitchen. "Where did the girl go?"

Then, Gen's voice, smaller. "I don't know."

Rupert's voice grew impossibly louder. It sounded like thunder, and rattled me just as deeply. "Stop lying! Do you really think I'm inclined to believe you after this? Do you have any *idea* the things I can do to you?"

I quickened my pace. Closer now. Only a few more steps, then–

I stumbled through the door.

Rupert looked back at me, visibly disheveled. His small quantity of hair was matted with sweat, and his clothing hung askew on his body. His gun was no longer in his waistband, but rather in his hand. Although he held it limply, his finger was noticeably positioned on the trigger.

He turned back to me, eyes overflowing with wild malice. He waved the gun in the air wildly, seeming almost delirious with rage. "Give me one reason I shouldn't use this on you," he slurred.

*Here. Now. I only want to be right here, right now.* I released the fabric, lifting the two stones upward so he could see them. "Because I have these."

He moved suddenly, pointing the gun directly at my chest.

Gen and Isaac gasped and began to lunge towards me, but I motioned for them to stop with my free hand.

Rupert's face hardened. "Give them to me. Tell me where you got them."

I sucked in a hard breath. *Here. Now. I only want to be right here, right now.* My hand trembled, causing the pieces to clatter against one another.

"I will," I said finally. "But you have to listen."

# CHAPTER NINETEEN

"I don't have to do anything. I've got this, remember?" Rupert moved both hands to hold the gun and aim it at me.

I licked my lips, "And I've got these," I lifted the stones again. "I could travel through time right now and you'd never see your stones again. So, if you want them, you do have to listen to me. Leo, too," I said, my voice shaking ever so slightly.

"Fine," Rupert said exhaustedly. "Leonard!" He pointed deliberately to the space beside him. Leo shuffled over and settled beside his father.

Once Leo was in place, my view of Gen and Isaac was blocked. My anxiety deepened.

"Now what?" Rupert said. "I'd really like to get this exchange over with." He adjusted his grip on the gun.

"First of all," I said, finally feeling my voice gaining some traction. "Give the gun to Peter. He won't shoot you, but I won't talk with it pointed at me."

"No."

"*Rupert,*" I said warningly. "Do you want me to talk or not?"

Relief exploded like tiny fireworks in my head when he relinquished the weapon to Peter. Peter took off his apron and wrapped the weapon in it.

Both Erindales turned back to me.

"What now?" Rupert said. His disheveled look had once seemed threatening, but now, without the gun, it seemed only pathetic. Despite this, I was still nervous. He seemed volatile, ready to explode at any moment. Now, his appearance acted as a warning label. *Contents under pressure.*

"I need you to picture something for me," I said.

"What does that have to do–"

"Look," I said, sounding braver than I felt. "Do you want the stones or not? Just do what I say."

Rupert crossed his arms. "Fine. Picture something. Am I supposed to go to my happy place?"

"Mock it and I won't give them to you," I said firmly. Peter smirked proudly. "Now, can I continue?" My voice stopped shaking. Rupert paused, then nodded. "Great. In order for you to understand this, you need to think about when they came from." I hesitated, then smiled. "1776. The year the stones were brought here." The stones grew warm in my hand. *Here. Now. I only want to be right here, right now.* They cooled off again.

"I don't need a history lesson, I need–"

"DO IT." The intensity of my voice startled even me. I coughed, then spoke softer. "Are you doing it?"

Rupert rolled his eyes, but nodded. "Yes. 1776. I still don't see what–"

"You don't have to understand now. You will. You just have to do it. Now close your eyes. Think of nothing but that year." *Here. Now. I only want to be right here, right now.*

"Is this some sort of trick?" Rupert said, opening his eyes. Leo's eyebrows were knit close together as he stared at me.

In that moment, I made my choice. "Catch."

I threw the stones. They missed their hands and hit the floor. Leo and Rupert fell onto their hands and knees, scrambling to collect the stones. Once they had them, they stood once more.

"You foolish girl," Rupert said. He tore Peter's apron away from him, and unwrapped the gun, pointing it back at me.

I held my breath.

"You've given us what we wanted. Now you have to listen to *me.*" His eyes looked like they were full of fire.

Then, suddenly, the stones began to glow. Rupert looked frantically down at his hands, then at Leo's. "What's happening? What did you do?"

He tried to shake the stone off, but it stuck to his palm.

He lunged toward me now, throwing the gun aside. My back screamed out as he pushed me into the wall. His breath was bitter and warm against my cheek as he spoke in a low whisper. "Don't think you've won," he growled, hands clasped around my shoulders like vices. "I will be back, and when I am I will not be so merciful. I will get what I want, and you will not be in my way."

He released me, and I slumped to the ground. I watched as he and Leo were jerked up by their wrists, disappearing into thin air.

I fell against the wall, finally feeling true relief. My breath came in heavy bursts. Isaac rushed toward me immediately.

"Are you okay? Did he hurt you? Oh my god, Kelsey, I was so scared…"

I reached up, grabbing his arm. "Isaac, calm down. I'm fine."

Gen squatted beside me, smiling. "You did amazing, Kelsey."

When I stood, Gen reached out, trying to steady me. "I'm fine," I said, brushing away her hand. "It's all fine."

Now, I truly believed my mantra. *Here. Now. I only want to be right here, right now.*

I walked over to Peter, who had yet to move from his chair. I couldn't hold back the question plaguing me since the beginning. "Why did you call us here?"

Peter looked surprisingly taken aback. "The truth?"

I took a deep breath. "Yes."

"Well," Peter said, "it was because I knew Rupert would come for me."

"Because of what you said in your journal?" Gen blurted.

Peter chuckled. "You found that too? I didn't expect that. Yes. I had been wanting to obtain apprentices for a long time, but I was never sure how I could make sure I got the right people. One must be cautious in ensuring power that begs to be used for bad intentions ends up in the hands of good intentioned people, after all. When I realized what Erindale was going to do, my plan fell into place." He chuckled again. "Granted, I thought I would've had a bit more time to train you three before he abducted me, but I wasn't that lucky."

"So you knew he'd take you?" I said, trying to keep my jaw from dropping.

"Essentially, yes."

"That is the craziest shot in the dark I have ever heard of," Isaac said.

Peter's laugh echoed off of the walls. "Yes, well, look at where we are now. It worked out, didn't it?"

I thought back through our journey. Part of me wanted to contest the idea. Worked out? With everything we'd been through it hardly felt like it. But, in a way, it had worked out. We had succeeded. I felt a surge of pride.

"So we passed?" Gen asked. "Do you consider us the right kind of people, I mean." Once the honors student always the honors student.

Peter broke into a wide smile. "With flying colors."

I chewed on my lip. "But I still don't understand."

Peter turned to me, looking thoughtful. "What don't you understand?"

"How this all works... The watches, I mean. If they worked in the same way the stones do, then we would have been able to come here right away. We were thinking about how much we wanted to be here almost all the time," I admitted shyly. "But they never took us here."

"But that first night," Gen interjected, "we got taken to 1811 just by putting them on. It doesn't make any sense."

Peter leaned back in his chair. When he finally spoke, we all leaned in close. "There are two key things that the watches do to restrain the power of the purple moons. The second is the reason Rupert was never able to use his watch."

"What are they?" Gen pressed.

"The first decreases the volatility. When the stones are placed within the watches, a release is required to allow them to function." He gestured to Gen.

She obediently removed her watch and handed it to him.

"See, here," he said, pointing at the small knob on the side of the watch. "When you twist it twelve times counter-clockwise…" he twisted as he spoke. On the twelfth turn, the watch began to glow a deep purple. "…It releases the purple moon. This is how you got to 1811 the first night. When I put the watches in the brick, they were already released."

"But we didn't know where we were trying to go. We weren't thinking of 1811," Gen countered.

"Oh, Genevieve," Peter said. "It's not always as superficial as that. If one is not thinking of a specific time, it takes you where you need to go. Where your *soul* needs to go. That's how I knew I could trust the three of you, unequivocally. You were meant to be there."

I fidgeted with the hem of my dress. My soul wanted to go there. The prospect seemed absurd but yet… Growing up in Gillonsville, the most exciting adventure the three of us ever got was going to a different ice cream shop than usual. Maybe what my soul needed was an adventure.

"That takes us to the second restriction," Peter said, not noticing my moment of reflection. He twisted the knob back, and the watch stopped glowing. "You can't travel alone." The watch was returned to Gen. "Two or more watches must be released, and the owners must desire to arrive in the same time. This, of course, is meant to ensure that people such as Rupert are unable to abuse the power. You must always have a second person with you. A conscience."

"But the journal said you would send Rupert back alone each night," Gen reasoned. "How could he get there?"

"He was never sent back by the watches," Peter said. "I would give him two of the stones. One to get home, one to go back. They only work once, outside of the watches. This is the one part of their power which the watches enhance. He would always come back, of course. Always wanted to keep working, or, as I learned, to keep obtaining power."

The room was quiet, but I didn't mind. I needed the moment.

The whole journey I had been unable to understand why Peter would have chosen us. *Us.* The honors student, the band geek, and, me. Not even interesting enough to earn a title. It seemed like a coincidence, a twist of fate which was never truly meant to be. But now, knowing that the watches knew we had it within us, within our souls… It didn't seem so random after all.

I felt proud, in a strange way.

"So what now?" Gen asked.

Peter looked up slowly, and I saw the same purple gleam in his eyes as the first night. "You go home."

Gen frowned. "Home? Why? Can't we stay with you?"

When Peter shook his head I could have almost sworn I saw a hint of sadness. "No. The danger has passed."

"But we want to keep learning!" Gen exclaimed. "There's so much we don't know!"

"And Rupert and Leo are still out there," Isaac added. "Will you be safe facing them alone?"

"I won't face them alone."

Peter's statement stung. So it wasn't only us. There were more apprentices. We weren't special, despite my earlier–

"I'll have you," Peter finished.

The burning in my chest receded. "What? How would we know if you need us again?"

"If I need you three again? You'll know. Trust me when I say I *will* call on you again, that's a promise I can make now. I'm not about to let the three of you slip through my grasp. But, that being said, you need to go home. You have a right to your lives. You have the right to be normal kids. As much as you can be, after this ordeal."

"But how will we *know*?" Gen urged.

"Keep a lookout," Peter said, characteristic twinkle returning to his eye. "I don't want you to waste your lives looking for my signal. Live fully, and deeply. As for me… I'll get back using a stone. You'll know me when you see me.

And you know the way back." He gestured to our watches. "Use it well."

Finally, Gen nodded in acceptance.

"So home, then?" Isaac asked. Gen and I met his gaze.

"I suppose," Gen said.

"Yeah." I couldn't help but smile.

A few moments later, Peter had guided us through the motions. Twelve counterclockwise turns. Thoughts of home.

I thought about the way the sun set behind my house, slowly disappearing behind the tall pines. I thought about Kelly's diner, and the funny pictures we took of each other as we sat within the booths. I thought of complaining about school and family, but secretly loving every moment. I thought about my life with my two best friends who sat beside me now, and would sit beside me then.

If I was some kind of hero, this would've been the point in the story where I said something terribly eloquent. I would've looked Peter right in the eye and shared some deep, philosophical sentiment.

But I wasn't a hero. I was a teenage girl who got roped into a ludicrous situation. I was just me. And in the true fashion of myself, I gave no dazzling final words. And despite what I expected, I was okay with that.

Maybe I didn't need to be a hero. Maybe that was the whole point.

So, when Peter smiled and said, "I'll see you three again," I responded like me. I took the word of somebody else above my own, and nodded. Blind agreement.

Gen took one of Isaac's hands. I held onto the other, then I held my breath.

"I'll see you later, then." Gen's parting declaration was no greater than mine. Even the honors student was at a complete loss for words.

Peter looked as if he was going to say something, but this time I was the one to shake my head. "Just tell me next time."

"It's been real, Peter," Isaac said.

The last thing I saw Peter Montague do before we were taken away was laugh. It seemed fitting. The watches took care of the rest. The not entirely uncommon sensation of being lifted up by my wrist began, and I closed my eyes against it.

# Epilogue

I sat alone in our usual booth at Kelly's diner. Gen and Isaac were supposed to have arrived five minutes before. It had been almost four months since our return from 1952. We were back in school, back to normal, really, or at least as close as we could be to it.

Every time the words 'back to normal' crossed my mind I had to fight the urge to laugh. Despite Peter's attempts to convince us, I knew that we were all constantly looking for a sign of his need for our return.

The bell hanging above the door tinkled as it was bashed by a rapid entrance. "Shoot!" a familiar voice yelled.

I looked up to see Isaac rushing through the door. He slumped down across from me, the faux leather squelching beneath him. He spoke breathlessly. "Sorry. I was reading the triplets the first Harry Potter and when I finished they wanted me to read them the first chapter of the second one and–"

"Isaac," I said, smiling. "It's fine."

Isaac nodded, and caught his breath for a moment. He grabbed a menu, although I knew he knew it by heart. He stared down at the little red font, then looked back up at me. "The usual, Kels?"

I shook my head, and Isaac looked surprised. "I thought I'd try something different."

"Speak for yourself," Isaac said with a grin. "Nothing beats the classics… Milkshakes and fries all the way."

When Gen came through the door it was far quieter than Isaac's entrance. She quickly made her way over sat down beside Isaac. Her hair was pulled into a tight ponytail.

"Homework?" I asked.

"Yes. How did you know?" Gen asked.

I shrugged, not saying that it was because I could see the tension draining out of her like sand in a colander as soon as she walked in.

"Well," I said, standing suddenly. "I think it's time for us to relax."

I got up and strode over to the still ancient looking jukebox. I produced a quarter from my pocket, and scanned through the list of songs until I found the one I wanted. I slid the quarter into the slot, and grinned back and Gen and Isaac.

"American Pie" began to seep through the speakers. A sense of freedom coursed through me, and I couldn't help but smile.

By the time the song reached it's chorus we were all on our feet, dancing around the diner as though no one else was there.

We were so lost in the music and our relief that we almost failed to notice the note which came tucked under our receipt.

Scrawling handwriting. Floral stationary.

*It is time.*

# ACKNOWLEDGEMENTS

So many people have helped me on this journey, and I truly believe it would be impossible to thank them all here by name. However, there are a few in particular I find it absolutely essential to mention. Firstly, endless thanks to my wonderful editor Selina McLemore. Thank you for taking the time to meet with me, and believing in the absurd dream of that almost-fifteen year old. This book could never have been what it is now without you. Your time and care in this process has made Kelsey, Gen, and Isaac's world all the more vibrant and meaningful, and I am forever grateful.

Thank you to Mr. Shane Kelly, for encouraging me to write this book in the first place. Without your encouragement and guidance in the early stages of this project, I truly believe it never would have happened. Additionally, thank you to Sebastian Marín-Quiros for helping me to write Gen's story with sensitivity and honesty. You've been a world of help in bringing her to life, and I am so incredibly grateful for it. Thank you to Amanda Slusser for reading the early, early drafts, and being excited about the story when, let's be honest, there wasn't really that much of a plot to it.

Endless thanks to my amazing cover designer, Allison Li (Alli May on 99Designs). You were astonishingly helpful in this process, and your vision did wonders for making this book everything it was able to become. Also, thank you to Wordzworth for doing the interior design for this novel. Your professionalism and knowledge has been instrumental in perfecting this book, and making it ready to be set out into the world.

Furthermore, thank you to my amazing parents, Kelly and Andrew Fennell, who have supported this project unconditionally since its inception. Without your continued support, love, and faith in the potential of this book, I never would have reached this point in my journey. I truly cannot thank you enough.

Finally, thank you to the nurses of OHSU Doernbecher's Infusion Center, Santo Randazzo, Beau Gambold, Liza St. James (and all of Columbia's 2018 Creative Writing: Masterclass in Fiction), Mr. John Bass, Mrs. Lindsay Allen, and each and every one of my fantastic friends, who have kept me going with their endless love and support over the last three years.

It's been a crazy journey to get here, and I couldn't have done it without all of these amazing people who gave their love and time to help me along the way.

Thank you.

# Author Bio

Claire Fennell is a sixteen year old high school student living with her parents and older sister in Lake Oswego, Oregon. The Watchmaker's Apprentice is her debut novel, but she has also been featured in Columbia University's Summer Program Literary Magazine "Interdimensional Train" and on Massachusetts General Hospital's "Neuropathy Commons." Besides writing, Claire also competes in speech and debate, and is Media Director for the LO Youth Leadership Council. She can be found seeking out the best coffee in the area, or burying herself in the stacks at Powell's.

Instagram: *@clairefennellwrites*
Email: *clairefennellwrites@gmail.com*